HER YELLOW TULIPS

A Tale of Love, Fate, and Covid

By

Fouzia Boutobza

"We write to taste life twice, in the moment and in retrospect."

Anais Nin

Dedication

To my mother, whose unwavering support and belief in me have been the guiding light to create my own path in life and never give up in the face of challenges.

And to my family, whose love has been the bedrock of my life.

Acknowledgments

I am grateful to Nicholas Horsburg & Hanane Daghour for their motivation & to Hilda Haghighi for her assistance.

About the Author

Fouzia Boutobza is a multifaceted Algerian author, mentor, and business leader whose diverse experiences have shaped her passion for exploring human behavior and relationships. With a background in computer engineering, Fouzia embarked on a career that led her to prominent roles within tech and energy corporations, including Fortune 100 companies like Microsoft and GE. Her work took her across the globe, from Asia to Africa, Europe, and the Middle East, exposing her to rich cultures and perspectives.

Fouzia's keen interest in human behavior and relationships remained a constant thread throughout her journey. She dug into studies of positive psychology and leadership, seeking to understand the intricacies of relational dynamics and personal growth. Her insights and experiences in various professional and cultural contexts were the foundation for her work as a mentor, guiding others on their paths to success and fulfillment.

While Fouzia initially shared her expertise through essays on business topics, her passion for literature classics and the human experience eventually inspired her to venture into the world of fiction.

With her debut book, Fouzia Boutobza establishes herself as a literary voice to watch, offering readers a thought-provoking exploration of the universal truths that bind us all together.

Table of Contents

Preface

In the land of strangers, where connections are fleeting, and emotions often take a backseat, dealing with feelings and relationships becomes crucial. With the rise of fantasy romance novels and superficial narratives about romantic relationships, expressing the workings & reflecting the authenticity of human emotions seem to be a vanishing art, lost in the noise of our modern world & social media. "Her Yellow Tulips" explores the complex, deep, and challenging dynamics in relationships in an attempt to help us reconnect to our inner voices, reflect on our choices, and navigate the layering & entanglement of our plethora of emotions...

From the complexity and depth that characterize mid-age love, the narrative interlaces various ingredients like a perfect dish. Passion, pride, guilt, innocence & empathy are intertwined to uncover the layers beneath the surface of diverse characters portraying personalities from our real world who often hide covert heroes, waiting to emerge through the tragedies of life.

Amid the challenges of the Covid-19 pandemic, the tale unfolds, emphasizing the blessings hidden in adversity. A pandemic that created a defining moment in our history but was an unprecedented opportunity for all to go back to our basic needs, valuing the simplest things in life that we often take for granted, and experience the bonds we have with our entourage, rediscovering the true meaning of human connections. "Her Yellow Tulips" serves as a reminder that love, a source of joy and suffering for so many, is not confined to age or circumstances, nor is it a predictable, methodical dynamic; it is a set of emotions and behaviors built on respect, trust, affection, passion, loyalty, and commitment that often happens unexpectedly and evolves evasively.

The story draws inspiration from timeless tales like "The Bridges of Madison County" & "Age of Innocence" and aims to share the blessings of tue love with younger generations. It encourages readers to embrace the multifaceted nature of romance, recognizing that it is just one ingredient in the complex recipe of life.

In a world filled with intense and negative stories, "Her Yellow Tulips" strives to bring a pause for reflection. Probing into the basics of human connections, portraying how individuals feel, process emotions, relate to each other, and handle challenging relationships. The narrative sheds light on our ability to experience authentic feelings & relate to one another with empathy, both of which are becoming less and less of a practice amidst the intensity of life. Reflection and insight-seeking moments are therefore encouraged.

This book is an invitation to connect with emotions, struggle with them, and find hope and smiles even in the face of hardship. The characters are diverse and relatable, each standing out in their unique way, leaving readers to ponder on their favorites.

Beyond the difficulties, "Her Yellow Tulips" is a compelling tale. The question is, will it be a sad ending, a happy beginning, or perhaps both? Let's embark on this journey and find out together.... Let's bridge the gap!

Chapter 1

New Blossoming

As the sun dipped below the horizon, the city began to quieten down. Hannah stepped out of her office building after wrapping up a grueling day, navigating through meetings and juggling deadlines, still maintaining her professional demeanor with vigor and precision.

As she walked down the busy street, she couldn't help but take in the sights and sounds of the city she had come to call home. The honking of cars, the hum of conversations, and the neon lights covered the cityscape in myriad colors—chaotic yet oddly comforting.

Hannah has always been a woman who thrived on challenges. She built her career from the ground up, overcoming obstacles that would have daunted most. Her journey to the position of Chief Technology Officer at Psynapse was a testament to her strength and independence. Alongside personal challenges, Hannah was fiercely dedicated to her work.

As she strode down the street, her phone rang, and the name on the caller ID was one she least expected. The mere sight of his name sent a chill down her spine. *What on earth could be the reason Seth was calling her?* They had parted ways for a reason, and she had fought hard to regain her independence and strength after their turbulent marriage.

Hesitating for a moment, she finally answered, "What do you want, Seth?" Her words were laced with caution. She had no plans of letting the past weaken her resolve.

Seth's voice, with unsettling heaviness, crackled through the phone. Hannah's suspicions stood corrected as soon as the first slurred word came out of his mouth.

"Hannah, I miss you, miss you soooo muuch." The words lurched out; clearly, he was under the influence of alcohol.

Hannah tightened her grip on the phone, her jaw clenched in frustration. She had dealt with Seth's erratic behavior during their marriage but was determined not to let it affect her now. She took a deep breath, attempting to maintain composure.

"Seth, it's late, and I have nothing to say to you. We've been over this. You need to get help and move on," she replied, her voice steady and unwavering.

But Seth wasn't ready to let go. He continued to mumble incoherent words, his tone oscillating between sadness and anger—a painful reminder of the past. Hannah couldn't help but feel a gush of rage.

"Miss you, Hannah, why won't you miss me?" Seth continued to slur.

Hannah's patience was wearing thin, and she finally snapped, "Seth, shut up."

Seth's tone turned hostile, his words venomous. "You think you're so much better than me, right? Always with your work and your 'independence.' You're nothing without me. You hear me…? You…"

Hannah's jaw tightened, her face flushing with disgust. She accelerated her pace as the passersby on the busy street glanced at her. Hannah was no stranger to adversity and had no intention of letting the intrusion ruffle her feathers.

"I can't do this now, Seth," she said firmly, cutting him off. "I need to go. Don't call me again." With that, she ended the call and took a deep breath, her resolve reaffirmed.

As she entered her apartment, she felt a weariness settled deep within her bones. She slumped onto her couch, letting out a long sigh.

The apartment, adorned with plants, bookshelves, and mementos from her philanthropic work, felt comforting and lonely at the same time. She looked at the withered tulips in the vase on the coffee table. The vibrant blooms she had bought just this morning were now drooping, their once-lively colors fading into a muted display.

Hannah's eyes fixed on the flowers as a thought crossed her mind. "I should have thrown them away," she mumbled. It was time to introspect.

As she contemplated the withered tulips, a more profound thought stirred in her mind. Her eyes drifted to the cityscape outside her window, a metropolis filled with millions of stories, each with its moments of vibrant beauty and inevitable decay. *Life is just like these tulips!*

The shrunken tulips served as a poignant reminder that life, like the once-fresh flowers, had its seasons. Moments of vitality gave way to periods of decline, followed by renewal and rebirth. Hannah's journey had followed a similar pattern. She had faced withering experiences and emerged stronger, her spirit renewed with each challenge.

***

The next morning, Hannah's alarm clock buzzed. It was 5:30 AM, and she rose with the same spirit that had seen her through many challenging days. The golden rays of the morning sun filtered through her curtains, casting a warm glow on her bed.

Hannah prepared a steaming cup of coffee, a familiar ritual that grounded her and provided the energy she needed for the day.

After savoring the first sip, she was set for her yoga class. As a believer in the power of physical activity to invigorate the mind and body, Hannah stepped out into the crisp morning air, her pace fast, transforming into a jog to her neighborhood yoga studio, three blocks away.

The city was still in the process of awakening. The streets were less crowded, and the air filled with a sense of serenity. Hannah felt the rhythm of her jog matching the beat of her heart; each step renewed a sense of strength.

After her early yoga class, Hannah, ready to tackle the day ahead, showered, dressed for work, and grabbed a quick bite. Her work at Psynapse was her calling; she had a sense of purpose each day. It was a place where her dedication and determination took tangible form.

Hannah's office building was a sleek and modern structure in the heart of the city. As the Chief Technology Officer at Psynapse, her responsibility was immense, and she embraced it with unyielding tenacity.

The bustling energy of her team greeted her as they prepared for another day of groundbreaking work. Her morning routine was like a well-orchestrated dance of meetings, emails, and decision-making, each task a testament to her leadership.

As she sat before her laptop with her team for their regular video conference call, colleagues from around the world appeared on the screen, eager to contribute to the day's discussions.

Amid the updates and technical jargon, one of the data scientists, Sam, spoke hesitantly, "I've been working on refining the algorithm," he began, his voice enthusiastic.

Hannah leaned forward as her brow furrowed with curiosity. "Go on, Sam. What have you found?"

Sam cleared his throat, his fingers nervously adjusting his glasses. "Well, I've been experimenting with a different input data set, and it seems to be improving our accuracy in detecting early signs of diseases. The initial results are promising."

Hannah's eyes lit up with interest. "That's fantastic, Sam. Let's dive into the details. Tell us more about how the new data set affects the results."

The rest of the day flowed seamlessly, with productive interactions. Hannah's calendar reminder chimed as the clock neared midday, marking a highly anticipated lunch date.

Cara had always been more than just a friend to Hannah; she was a confidante, a kindred spirit who had entered Hannah's life like a breath of fresh air—a window that had never before opened for her. They shared a deep love for the arts—from opera to vintage films, and often attended art exhibitions and museums together. Their connection extended beyond cultural interests; they had both embarked on a journey towards holistic living.

Cara had recently transitioned from a successful tech startup to a simpler, more rounded life. It was a decision that had baffled many of her acquaintances, but Hannah understood. It was about finding balance—a deeper connection with life.

Hannah's favorite café was 'The Cozy Café,' but the vegan café Cara had chosen for their lunch was new in town, reaffirming her commitment to a healthier existence. Hannah arrived promptly after finishing her work engagements, excited to catch up with her closest friend.

With warm smiles, they exchanged a hug. Their bond was palpable, the kind of friendship that transcended distance and time, built on shared experiences, and their unwavering support for each other—a rarity to treasure.

Cara looked at Hannah curiously as they settled at their table. "So, how was your trip with that guy you recently met? What was his name again?" Cara asked.

Hannah's eyes twinkled as she spoke. "His name is David Barnes, and he's not just about tech; he cares for the environment, recycles, and, by the way, we went hiking and had a great time. He's been divorced twice, you know!"

Cara raised an eyebrow, her interest piqued. "Two divorces? That's intriguing. And?"

Hannah picked a piece of lettuce from her salad bowl and bit gracefully. "Well, my dear, he's been quite over the top. He gifted me a diamond necklace and cradled my ring finger in his hand. He even asked if I wanted a matching ring to go with it."

Cara chuckled, a hint of sarcasm in her smile. "You know, they say the third time's the charm."

Hannah's expression turned thoughtful. "It's been two years since my divorce, Cara, and I've met my fair share of men. Many have been interested, but I can't feel any real connection."

Cara leaned in, her voice gentle. "Have you thought about what you want in a partner, hon? Maybe you're not finding the right fit because you haven't figured yourself out yet."

Hannah replied with a firm gaze. "I know what I want. Someone who is emotionally intelligent and sensitive and understands me more deeply. But all the men I've met lately seem shallow and superficial. None of them have resonated with me in any way."

Cara's eyes offered support. "Well, maybe you need to give it some time. You can't force a connection. What's important is to remember that you don't need anyone to complete you. You're amazing on your own."

Hannah smiled and nodded in agreement. "I will turn 40 next year, Cara, and I just feel like an alarm bell always rings at the back of my mind."

Cara stopped chewing her piece of grapefruit and fixed her gaze on her friend. "What kind of alarm bell? Don't tell me that an intelligent, accomplished woman like you has been pulled into the pressure of having children by the hypercritical society?"

Hannah's expression showed a hint of sadness. "That's not what I meant. You know how I spent all those years with Seth; I wanted kids. It was his unstable, toxic behavior that made me decide otherwise. But now, I feel like maybe I'm missing out on something. Like a void in my core. I know I would make a good mother, but in my 40s, I might not stand a chance."

Stroking the rim of her glass thoughtfully, Cara said, "And you will find that when the time is right. I think time is still on your side. Overthinking wouldn't help. Maybe you must let destiny take care of things for a while."

Hannah's face suddenly brightened. "Yeah, that's exactly what I thought. I'm trying not to overthink and let things take their natural course."

Cara smiled, feeling reassured by her friend's words. *Aren't words powerful!* She took a deep breath and returned to the moment, trusting the journey ahead would be smooth.

After lunch, Hannah returned to her office. The afternoon was a whirlwind of pitch meetings with clients, Team calls, and ironing out details with investors. Hannah finally wrapped up her work engagements as the sun descended below the horizon.

A sense of solitude enveloped her as she walked back to her apartment. Her thoughts of the past and longing for a deeper connection crept into her mind. She took a deep breath, determined not to let these feelings overwhelm her.

Just a few blocks away from her apartment, a cozy flower shop caught her eye. The doorbell chimed as she entered, and the shop owner, a friendly woman in her sixties, greeted her with a warm smile.

"Hello, dear. How can I help you today?"

Hannah's eyes rested on a bouquet of fresh tulips, their vibrant colors whispering hope and a new sense of purpose. She reciprocated with an equally warm smile and said, "I'll take these tulips, please."

With the tulips in her hand, she left with a sense of tranquility. The simple act of buying fresh flowers felt like a significant step toward revivifying her life.

In her apartment, she removed the withered tulips from the vase, their petals frail and lifeless, and replaced them with the fresh tulips she had just purchased. As she arranged them, she couldn't help but smile, appreciating the beauty and vitality of the new blooms.

Hesitantly, she opened her laptop, and after a moment of contemplation, she pressed the 'enter' key. Her dating profile had been dormant for a while but was now updated with a recent photo and a few revisions to her aspirations.

As she gazed at the fresh tulips on her table, their vibrant colors mirroring her newfound hope, a joyful smile played on her lips as she thought about the endless possibilities that awaited her arms. *Maybe, just like these fresh flowers, her life would bloom again.*

Chapter 2

Ben

Hannah was at her desk, her fingers typing away on the keyboard with precision. The office hummed with the energy of progress, the sun bathing the room in warm light through the windows. As she reviewed reports and plans, her mind focused entirely on the task; her phone chimed with a message notification. Hannah frowned, not expecting any important messages at this hour. She glanced casually and almost jumped as she saw the dating website's icon. The notification was from the unknown.

With her eyes wide, Hannah scanned the message; her curiosity piqued yet tinged with caution. She shook her head, unsure what to make of it. She tried refocusing on work, but this time, it was compromised. The allure of the mysterious message and the stranger continued to tug at her thoughts.

You stand out like a desert rose,

Look so beautiful. I wish to see you up close,

You have put me under your spell,

If you don't reciprocate, I wish you well.

Hannah couldn't help but think about the message incessantly. The poetic lines played like a haunting melody in her mind.

But if you would like, I can show you a good time,

A classy woman like you deserves everything fine,

I am hoping you won't be a tease,

Here's my number, call me if you please.

She groaned with frustration, realizing she couldn't concentrate with the stranger hanging over her head. There was something in his words… To regain focus, she put her phone in the desk drawer and closed it, hoping to keep it out of sight but not out of mind. Yet, the appeal of the unknown and the poetic lines continued to resurface in her mind like a riddle she couldn't resist solving. *Too intriguing to resist!*

Hannah eventually decided to face it—the mysterious message. She sneakily opened her desk drawer and retrieved her phone. Her fingers were trembling with anticipation as she unlocked the screen.

Her eyes broadened as she saw the name "Ben" on the message. It wasn't just any message; the lines seemed familiar. *Who is this stranger who had crafted those poetic lines? Or was he a stranger!* She hesitated a moment before tapping to read the message. The acquainted lines appeared on the screen.

As Hannah reread the lines, her heart fluttered in her chest. The words held a mesmerizing charm, and she couldn't help but feel a connection to the person behind the message—A uniqueness to Ben's approach that set him apart.

Hannah started to type a reply, eager to see his reaction.

Her fingers danced across the screen as she composed her response. She wanted to capture her sense of intrigue and the mystery Ben had woven with his words.

Your message has caught my attention in a way that's hard to explain. It's unlike anything I've come across on this platform. I appreciate the artistry in your words. How about we start with a conversation? You can call me a traditionalist, but I'd like to get to know you a bit before we jump the gun. What's the story behind that poetic soul of yours?

She hit the send button as she waited for Ben's response. The conversation felt like a breath of fresh air, a glimmer of something exceptional on the horizon.

Hannah's contemplations were consumed by the enigmatic stranger who had entered her life through a dating app.

Amid her day-to-day responsibilities at the office, the rhythmical lines he'd sent her kept reverberating in her mind like a frequent melody:

You stand out like a desert rose,

Look so beautiful; I wish to see you up close,

You have put me under your spell,

If you don't reciprocate, I wish you well,

But if you would like, I can show you a good time,

A classy woman like you deserves everything fine,

I am hoping you won't be a tease,

Here's my number, call me if you please.

Her mind kept wandering between work assignments and fantasyland. The mysterious stranger had woven his enchanting words like magic into her world.

A colleague, Zoe, couldn't help but notice the change in Hannah's demeanor. Her usual focus was replaced with a faraway look in her eyes. She seemed distracted. Concerned, Zoe approached her.

"Hey, Hannah, you seem a bit zoned out today. Everything okay?" Zoe asked, furrowing her brows in genuine concern.

Hannah's heart raced as she was caught off guard. She quickly regained her composure, not wanting to reveal her sweet secret.

"Oh, hey, Zoe," she stammered, "I'm just feeling a bit under the weather today, but I'll be fine, don't you worry."

Zoe nodded, though still concerned. "Well, if you need anything, just let me know. I'm here for you."

Hannah managed a weak smile and thanked Zoe for her concern. As Zoe returned to work, Hannah drifted back to bask in the glory of Ben's message.

Hannah's phone lit up; another notification and her heart skipped a beat as she saw Ben's name on the screen. She rapidly unlocked her phone, and the message read:

Dear Hannah,

Your response made my day. I'm thrilled that you appreciated my words. Honestly, I've always been a bit of a romantic at heart. Words paint pictures in my mind, and when I read your profile, I couldn't help but be inspired.

I'd love to have a conversation with you, Hannah. The story behind those lines is a tale, and I'm eager to share it with you. How about we start with a phone call? I promise I'm a much better conversationalist than a poet.

Hannah's lips curved into a soft smile as she read the message repeatedly. There was a distinctive warmth in his words that put her at ease, and the idea of hearing his voice held a certain pull, and she already felt butterflies going nuts in her stomach. She began to type her reply, her fingers dancing tenderly over the screen, as did her heart in her ribs.

Ben,

Your willingness to share the story behind your poetry intrigues me even more. How about we keep it mysterious and exchange text messages for now? We can get to know each other through our words. Words have weight when so light… What do you think?

She pressed 'send' and leaned back in her chair, her heart racing. The unfolding connection felt like a thrilling adventure she was more than ready to embark on.

As Hannah and Ben exchanged text messages, she opened up in a way she hadn't experienced before. As if there was an unspoken understanding between them, a unique connection that allowed her to share her thoughts, fears, and dreams without reservation. Ben's words were a soothing balm that felt like a familiar stranger, a genuine connection she's been missing for so long.

Their conversations deepened, delving into topics beyond the superficial. They talked about their families, upbringing, and experiences that shaped them into the people they were.

Hannah: *I must admit, I'm looking forward to our daily conversations. It's been a while since I felt this way.*

Hannah sensed vulnerability wash over her as she sent the message. She hadn't felt this eager to talk to someone in a long time, and while it excited her, she was frightened, too.

Ben: *I feel the same way, Hannah. You're incredibly easy to talk to. I cherish our conversations.*

Reading Ben's words, Hannah's heart skipped a beat, and she couldn't help but smile as she typed back.

Hannah: *Tell me more about your family. You mentioned they were distant. What was it like growing up?*

With a sense of curiosity, Hannah's eyes glued to her phone screen as she awaited Ben's response. She genuinely wanted to know this person.

Ben: *It's a complicated story, but I'd love to share it with you. My family prioritized duty over emotional connection, leaving me yearning for something more.*

Hannah could sense the depth of emotion in his words. She admired his willingness to open up.

Hannah: *I'm here to listen, and I'm glad you're comfortable sharing with me.*

Her words carried a sense of reassurance, a promise that she was there to support him. She had always been a good listener and looked forward to hearing Ben's story.

Ben: *Thank you. It means a lot to have someone who truly understands. You've brought warmth and light into my life.*

Ben's gratitude touched Hannah's heart, a man she had only met online. And yet, his words resonated with hers, making her feel valued.

As time passed, they got closer. Hannah never let him feel he needed to walk on eggshells around her. On the contrary, she made him feel like he could express his true self without fear of being judged.

Ben's need for emotional connection and desire to build a meaningful relationship mirrored Hannah's desires. They found solace in each other's words and began to believe they might have found something truly special, something that had the potential to change both of their lives forever. As their connection developed, Hannah's hope for the future seemed real.

The days turned into weeks, but they hadn't yet admitted their feelings for each other, although even a stranger could tell they were falling in love.

The relationship was like a slow burn, a steady flame that refused to flicker out. Each day, their bond grew stronger, and the walls they had built around their hearts began to crumble, exploring uncharted territories of emotions and vulnerability.

Hannah and Ben soon became soulmates, knowing a unique and deep connection transcending the boundaries of ordinary romance. It was as if they had known each other in a past life and now, in this lifetime, were finding their way back to each other.

They began to read each other's thoughts without the need for words. Their conversations knew no boundaries: love, life, and things close to their hearts. The closeness left them in awe of the serendipity that had brought them together like puzzle pieces that fit perfectly—two souls reuniting after a long and arduous journey. As if the universe had conspired to connect them, they couldn't help but feel fate did it.

Hannah and Ben continued to share their dreams, thoughts, and innermost fears with no inhibitions. It wasn't just talking; their souls bonded with each other. It was a level of emotional intimacy that neither of them had ever experienced—vulnerable yet secure.

Chapter 3

The Red Flag

Hannah was a creature of habit, her life meticulously organized by a strict daily routine. Yoga kept her sanity, given a workday filled with meetings, presentations, and deadlines. Her job was fulfilling, and she always found time for her creative pursuits, channeling her passion for art and beauty. Learning something new was a constant joy for her.

Life took a sudden turn on an ordinary day at work. During a meeting, Hannah was struck by a sharp pain in her chest. She initially dismissed it as stress, but the pain intensified. An odd sensation gripped her throat, making it difficult to breathe. It felt almost like a panic attack, something she had never encountered before. Anxiety overcame Hannah as she recognized something was seriously not right. She excused herself from the meeting and hurried to the emergency room. The fear was overwhelming. As she waited for the doctors, she felt vulnerable.

Hannah's fear and anxiety intensified as she experienced troubling symptoms. Uncertainty loomed large as she awaited the diagnosis, her mind fraught with worries about her health and future. The night unfolded with a rollercoaster of emotions, from dread to hope, until the root cause of her condition was revealed: food intolerance rather than a more serious ailment. As she lay in her hospital bed, Hannah's perspective on life underwent a profound transformation. The brush with mortality forced her to confront her priorities and reevaluate her choices. Amidst the chaos of medical procedures and tests, her thoughts drifted to Ben, whose comforting presence lingered in her mind. She realized the depth of her attraction to him, stirring a desire for honesty and authenticity in their relationship.

She spent the next few days recuperating in bed, appreciating the time off work. In the quiet moments of reflection, Hannah thought, *How frequently we overlook the value of life until we are confronted with its fragility.* In her mind, Hannah made resolutions to savor life's simple pleasures and pursue her deepest desires. The experience became a catalyst for embracing life with renewed vigor, determined not to squander any more time on trivialities.

Meanwhile, Ben, unaware of her health scare, was concerned as he anxiously awaited word from her. It has been 24 hours, and no text from her. This silence created a sense of alarm in his mind as he grappled with the fear of losing her. The intensity of his emotions surprised him, leading him to acknowledge the strength of his feelings for Hannah and the significance of their connection.

The frightening incident suddenly transformed Hannah's perspective on life as it took a 180-degree turn in her mind. She decided to slow down, cherishing the simple pleasures of life often conveniently ignored. She also couldn't overlook the fact that she felt attracted to Ben. She yearned for the day when she could be honest about her feelings, curious to know if he felt the same way.

The night in the emergency room seemed to have come as a blessing in disguise that had made Hannah confront her mortality, shifting her outlook on everything. She was now motivated to savor life to the fullest and not squander any more time.

As Hannah drifted off to sleep, her thoughts naturally gravitated toward Ben. She wondered if he was thinking about her and how sharing that night in the ER with him would affect their relationship. The very thought of it was daunting. Amid uncertainty and fear, Hannah and Ben's shared experience was paving the way for greater honesty and vulnerability in their newfound understanding.

While Hannah was contemplating the significant changes in her life, Ben couldn't help but feel a sense of anxiety. He had been texting her, pouring his thoughts and feelings into his messages, longing and concern evident, but she hadn't responded.

"Hey, Hannah, are you okay?" Ben texted.

Minutes turned into hours, and still, no response from Hannah. Ben's anxiety grew, and he sent another one, "Please, let me know you're okay."

Ben couldn't shake off the uneasy feeling as the day wore on. His text now more anxious, "Hannah, I'm worried about you. Please text me when you're free."

The silence on the other end was deafening, and Ben's thoughts were racing with worry. He couldn't believe how concerned he felt for someone he hadn't met! It was a moment of realization that he'd begun to care about Hannah deeply and couldn't bear the thought of something happening to her. The uncertainty gnawed at him, and he anxiously awaited her reply, hoping to hear her voice and know she was all right.

As the sun's rays gently streamed into her room the following day, Hannah felt anxious and excited about her bond with Ben. She couldn't deny the influence he had on her life. The thought of opening up to him about her vulnerability seemed terrifying and yet liberating.

She picked up her phone and started typing:

"Hey Ben, sorry to have you worried. I want to share something with you. I had a false alarm concerning my health recently. It was frightening, but simultaneously, it made me realize how precious life is and how important it is to cherish our connections with people. I want you to know that our conversations have brought much joy into my life, and I look forward to meeting you soon. Let's cherish every moment, and I look forward to a brighter future together."

After sending the message, Hannah felt relief. She hoped Ben would understand and that their bond would strengthen. As she set her phone down, she couldn't help but smile, feeling that life, as unpredictable as it is, was always full of unexpected twists that she was ready to embrace. She had a feeling—the journey ahead would be fascinating.

Her phone chimed.

"Dear Hannah, I'm sorry to hear about your health scare. I can't help but feel worried. I wish I could have been there with you during that challenging time. Please take care of yourself, and if you need anything or someone to talk to, I'm just a phone call away."

***

Days passed, and Hannah looked forward to the moments she could talk to Ben. They would discuss everything from their favorite books to their dreams and aspirations. Even though they had never met in person, Hannah felt a sense of comfort, and their text conversations flowed effortlessly.

Monday turned out to be Hannah's lucky day; Ben called her for the first time.

She could hear the charm in his voice as he tried to make her smile with his witty jokes and smooth talking. Hannah couldn't help but be drawn to him. Ben seemed to know that Hannah was a woman who wouldn't waste her time on just anyone, so he had to put his *best efforts* into courting her.

They delved deeper into each other's likes, dislikes, and personal stories. Hannah shared her deep passion for the opera, a form of art that resonated with her profoundly.

On the 24th of January, Hannah's birthday, she received a delightful surprise from Ben. A bouquet of her favorite yellow tulips and a box of exquisite Belgian chocolates arrived at her doorstep, accompanied by a note with two tickets for the opera. It was a thoughtful gesture, a testament to how well Ben was getting to know her.

Hannah, however, didn't want to feel pressured into starting a relationship with a man she had never met. She didn't like to compromise on her values.

Nevertheless, Ben was persistent. He continued to surprise her with his poetic words and kind gestures; each effort was a step forward to winning her heart. Hannah was hesitant; a delicate dance of resistance prevailed in her mind, trying to protect herself from the whirlwind of emotions that Ben stirred within her. *Was it the fear of the past or just the unknown?* She couldn't say.

Despite her doubts, Hannah couldn't deny the charm and genuine kindness that Ben exuded. As time passed, the walls she had built around herself began to crumble, and she found herself mysteriously drawn to him. In an unprecedented move, Hannah allowed herself to make an exception for Ben.

Their connection, while unconventional, felt natural and effortless. It was as if their hearts decided to take the lead, bypassing the logical reservations that typically governed Hannah's decisions. She was taking a leap of faith into uncharted territory, and the journey promised nothing short of extraordinary.

A unique connection based on mutual respect, admiration, and intellectual stimulation was almost like a dream. Despite contrasting personalities, they found relief in each other's company. With all guards down, they were like two innocent children enjoying life's simple joys.

As a firm, intelligent, and independent woman, Hannah delayed uncovering her accurate self. Thanks to the scars from before, she was being protective of her heart, cautious of her pace. However, Ben's intellect and charm broke down her emotional dividers over time, encouraging her to open up to him.

Ben was a pragmatic man with a fragile ego. He often appeared cold and distant, but with Hannah, he felt a zest of warmth and passion that he wasn't familiar with. Hannah could almost sense his smile and joy whenever he talked to her. It was like magic.

Their conversations, filled with laughter, wit, and playful flirting, would brighten their nights. The depths of deliberations were furthering from just liking.

The telepathic bond carrying mystery and the passion igniting their deepest desires made them ever more explicit about their feelings.

Ben became a regular part of her dreams at night, and in her heart, she knew he was also dreaming of her. The vibe they shared was intense, filling them with wonder and awe.

One night, Ben's voice grew solemn as they spoke on the phone. "Hannah," he began, "I need to tell you something. I've never felt so deeply connected to anyone in my life. You've opened up a part of me I didn't know existed. Talking to you and getting to know you has changed everything for me," he said in a hoarse tone, meaning every word he spoke.

Hannah's heart began to race as she absorbed the weight of Ben's confession. Her voice slightly quivered as she replied, "Ben, the feeling is mutual. I've never experienced anything like this before, either. It's like we've stumbled upon something truly special beyond words."

It was a moment in time…

Their connection deepened even further. They continued sharing their thoughts, hopes, and dreams, oblivious of the world, basking in the glory of their newfound, enchanting reality. They found the perfect confidant in each other, offering unwavering emotional support, lifting each other during moments of doubt, and providing comfort in sadness.

They both felt they were meant to be together and yet hesitated to take the next step, afraid of getting hurt and terrified of what is now and what would happen next.

Ben felt a shift in his mindset as if she was transforming him almost hypnotically; he was no longer the distant and aloof man he once was, but instead, a passionate, romantic poet and a pure, delightful lover fresh out of a fairytale. Ben was absorbed by the faraway, exceptional woman that Hannah was, and he started pouring his heart out to her in a way he never thought he could.

One night, Ben said, "You are an enchanting woman, Hannah. I just wanted to ensure you know that already!" His voice was soft and reassuring. "You have awakened a passion so deep in me that I cannot contain the feeling of being away from you."

Hannah felt her face flush with blood. She had never experienced such a feeling with anyone; it was as if she had just become alive. "You make me feel alive, Ben. Before knowing you, I was just living," she said tenderly. "I never imagined I could feel this way about someone. But you proved me wrong, and I'm glad you did."

***

As the pandemic began to spread worldwide, forcing people to be distant from each other, Hannah and Ben felt closer than ever. Separated by distance, they found refuge in one another. Ben would wake Hannah up with his beautiful and exciting texts every morning and kiss her goodnight with his poetic note every night. He had the gift of the gab, and Hannah was his muse.

As the world was discovering a new order thanks to COVID-19, Hannah was reviving her zest for love and life, thanks to Ben.

The COVID-19 pandemic ushered in unprecedented changes that profoundly impacted people's lives. For Hannah, the lockdown brought an overwhelming sense of loneliness. Her once-vibrant social life came to a screeching halt, leaving her confined to the four walls of her home, as was the story of all people alive. The daily routine that used to excite her became monotonous, and the desire for human connection grew stronger by the day. COVID-19 was there in school, and the classes were mandatory.

Like many others, the limitations began to take a toll on Ben's mental health. Feelings of anxiety and stress became his frequent companions as he grappled with finding effective ways to cope with the situation.

Nonetheless, amidst the chaos and volatility, a loving association was thriving between Ben and Hannah. Phone calls and text messages were the only means to cultivate a profound and meaningful bond. Their longing for the day they could finally meet in person had some time before bearing fruit. Each passing day would augment the bitter-sweet pain of physical absence.

Regrettably, the COVID-19 lockdown came with different plans, making it impossible for them to take their relationship to the next level. The uncertainty of when they might be able to meet face-to-face weighed heavily on both of them, and they contended with the fear that life might never return to normal, casting doubts on their dreams of finally being together.

But with the uncertain circumstances lingering around, the real question was, for how long?

Chapter 4

The Beginning

The world was wrestling with the pandemic, but Ben's desire to see Hannah grew stronger each day. Besides the miles between New Jersey and New York, COVID was the actual distance. Just an hour and a half away and yet miles apart. As they say, *"so near yet so far..."*

Ben yearned to meet Hannah in person, and he revisited the idea in his mind over and over again. Twice, he had mustered the courage to propose plans for their long-anticipated meeting, but Hannah wanted to be careful.

Ben was now suspicious that perhaps she was avoiding meeting him.

His passion for Hannah was almost bordering on obsession. While his feelings were deep and genuine, he couldn't help but feel that his intensity might have pushed Hannah away, hence the delay in the prospect of their first face-to-face encounter.

The fear of meeting someone who meant so much to her after so long was a heavy burden she carried.

What if he doesn't live up to her expectations, and she discovers a person too far from the image he portrayed? She couldn't risk that.

She dreaded her dreams crashing down, but clearly, *Ben couldn't wait any longer.*

He thought about her every waking hour, but he also couldn't ignore the thought that she was just as nervous about meeting him as he was.

Despite the boundaries of the pandemic, Ben couldn't help but feel frustrated that he hadn't been able to see Hannah yet. He had been waiting for this moment for so long, and the delay was becoming unbearable.

One evening, as Ben was staring out of his clinic window, lost in thoughts, his phone rang. It was Hannah. His heart skipped a beat as he answered.

"Hi, Hannah, how are you?" Ben tried to sound casual.

"I'm good, thanks for asking, Ben. I know I've been busy lately, but I wanted to check in and see how you're doing," Hannah replied.

"I'm doing okay, just been busy with work," Ben said, trying not to sound desperate.

There was a brief moment of silence before Hannah spoke again. "Ben, I have to be honest with you. I'm nervous about meeting you in person. I know we've bonded, but finally meeting you in person scares me."

Ben felt a wave of relief wash over him. He wasn't the only one feeling nervous. "I understand, Hannah. It's perfectly natural to feel anxious. I feel the same way," he said.

There was another pause before Hannah said, "But I still want to meet you. I need a little more time to prepare myself; perhaps that's what COVID wants, too," she said.

"Take all the time you need, Hannah. I'll be here waiting for you," Ben replied, his voice filled with sincerity.

***

As the days turned into weeks, the anticipation and impatience for their first meeting only grew. Hannah felt herself falling for Ben, and her emotions swelled with each passing day. She could sense that this wasn't just infatuation; it was far-reaching. The messages and calls had become a lifeline, a way to bridge the physical distance that separated them.

Their conversations continued like an unending dance, a waltz of words and emotions. Hannah shared stories she had never told anyone, and Ben reciprocated with equal honesty.

Late-night conversations became the norm, they voiced the soundtrack of their blossoming relationship.

And then, one evening, as they talked about their childhood memories, Hannah's voice quivered as she shared a long-buried pain from her past. Ben felt his heart aching for her.

Hannah couldn't help but wonder if she had finally found the love she had been searching for, would she have the courage to say those three little words that held so much power, "I love you."

Hannah had reached a point where she couldn't bear it. She decided it was time to step forward to see if their chemistry had weight. It was time to bring Physics into play.

Her heart pounded with excitement as she dialed Ben's number. The phone rang, and her anticipation grew.

Moments later, a young girl's enthusiastic voice exclaimed on the other side, "Dad!" The surprise in Hannah's reaction was unambiguous.

Suddenly, the sound of the phone shuffling broke through, followed by Ben's voice, tinged with gentle scolding. "Emma, you know you're not supposed to answer my phone calls like that."

Hannah's heart sank for a moment; confusion and anxiety flooded her. But then, a soft, whispered voice reached and sang her name, "Hannah."

Tears welled up in Hannah's eyes as emotions swirled within her. A dash of sadness washed over her. She had to end the call immediately to gather her thoughts and feelings. Without a word, she disconnected the call, with a myriad of questions unanswered in her heart. The sense of unease was beyond her.

Emma into their equation had taken her by surprise. She needed time to process the unforeseen and wondered how to navigate the situation.

Hannah's mind raced with a whirlwind of emotions. She couldn't help but second-guess her decision to engage in this long-distance relationship. The presence of a young girl in Ben's life didn't quite fit in her dreams and had raised a series of nagging questions.

Was Ben married or hiding something? The thought began to cloud her judgment. She felt like a fool, allowing herself to become emotionally invested without knowing the complete picture. The uncertainty of the situation weighed heavily on her.

She needed answers, but her emotions were in turmoil, and her thoughts were a tangled web of concerns.

Hannah watched as Ben's name flashed on her phone's screen, the ringtone chiming softly in the room. Her heart raced between the desire to answer and the need for space to collect her thoughts. Amid her emotional mayhem, she decided not to respond. The call eventually went to voicemail.

The sudden revelation about Ben's daughter had caught her off guard.

She attended the second call and stayed quiet.

There was a long pause before Ben finally spoke. "Hannah, I have something important to tell you," he said, his voice shaking.

Hannah's mind raced with possibilities.

Before Hannah could voice her confusion, Ben's following words struck her like lightning. "I'm married, Hannah," he declared, his voice weighed down by the burden of secrecy. "I kept it from you, fearing it would change everything between us. But I can no longer hide the truth."

Hannah's world spun before her eyes. Her heart pounded against her chest, betrayal, and disbelief blurring her feelings.

Married?

How was this possible?

Her mind was trying to piece together the fragments of shattered trust.

She had never even considered the possibility that Ben would be married. It shook her to the core, and she couldn't even bring herself to speak. All she could do was listen as Ben continued to talk, his voice sounding increasingly desperate.

"I completely understand if you decide to end the relationship at this point, and I would respect your choice. These are complicated circumstances; you don't have to involve yourself."

But Hannah couldn't hear him anymore.

She felt like she was going to be sick. She couldn't believe that the man she had been falling for had been married all along.

Hannah took a deep breath before responding.

"Ben, how could you not tell me?" she asked, her voice a mere whisper, trembling with emotion.

There was a long pause on the other end of the line before Ben finally spoke.

"I'm sorry, Hannah. I should have told you earlier. I was scared that if I did, you wouldn't want to talk to me anymore," he said regretfully.

"That's not the point, Ben. You kept me away from the truth. All those intimate conversations we had, all those shared moments; they were built on a lie," Hannah said, her voice rising with anger.

Ben's voice trembled with guilt. "I know, and I'm deeply sorry. Deceiving you was never my intention. It's just ... finding the right time was so hard," he confessed as if each word weighed heavily on his conscience.

"I need some time to think about all of this, Ben. I feel so angry and disappointed that I can't even talk to you right now," Hannah said and hung up.

Her heart was in ruins, battered by the crushing weight of betrayal. She had invested every ounce of trust in Ben, believing he was her destined partner. But now, standing amidst the debris of her devastated dreams, she was engulfed in a storm of emotions—drama, disappointment, confusion, and seething anger. The revelation hit her deeply, leaving her in a daze. *Could she ever love again after this?* A swirl of chaos was going in her mind, each memory now tainted with the bitter sting of betrayal.

"Dad!" One word changed her. Ben's lie had changed everything.

The world was so different just moments ago!

As she sat alone in her apartment, Hannah couldn't help but wonder how she could have been so wrong about Ben. How could she have let herself fall for someone who was already taken? How can she not know?

The realization left her feeling lost, *unsure of what to do next.*

Days passed as Hannah retreated, and Ben couldn't help but feel bewildered and abandoned. It was as if the air around him was thick with unspoken emotions, and he yearned for her more than ever.

***

Hannah sat alone in her favorite spot by the window, her thoughts racing like a turbulent river. The dilemma haunting her for weeks still lingered in her mind. *Should she call Ben and confront him for betraying her?*

The pain of deception and the depth of their connection burdened her heart. She felt her emotions were delving into a deep slumber. She had always believed in morality, and Ben's initial omission had crushed her ideal. Time progressed, but she failed to conquer the void his absence had created.

She knew their connection was authentic, or at least it felt that way; their conversations had touched her in ways no one else had. Something undeniably unusual about Ben had drawn her in, something she couldn't simply forget.

Hannah couldn't help but wonder if there was a way to bridge the gap.

She gazed out the window, recalling their conversations, shared dreams, and forged connections. She had always trusted her instincts, and her heart told her something was worth salvaging here.

She took a deep breath and decided to confront her lingering feelings. She wanted to seek clarity on their story to be sure if it was just a chapter before she could think more…

She dialed his number, and Ben immediately picked up but stayed quiet. Hannah sighed, "Say something, Ben."

"I am so sorry, Hannah."

Hannah could hear the pain in his voice as he continued to share his emotions. His words painted a picture of a man torn between his responsibilities as a father and the intolerable cargo of a hopeless marriage. The guilt he felt for his daughters' sake was deep.

Ben's voice quivered. "Hannah, it's been an endless struggle trying to keep up this facade for the sake of my family. I love my daughters more than anything in the world, but I can't continue living in this misery. I know it's not fair to anyone, you, my wife, and especially my daughters. I'm sorry, Hannah. But my marriage has gone sour. Maybe Sarah and I weren't meant for each other, and now I have to stay in this relationship just for the sake of my daughters. Please try to understand. This marriage doesn't mean anything; it's a dead flower. I'm only watering it because of my daughters," Ben sighed and continued.

"I have longed for a love like this for a very long time, Hannah, and you're the only person who's gotten this close to me and showed me what it's like to be truly loved. Forgive me, Hannah… Please tell me this doesn't end here. It tore me apart every time we talked, and I didn't dare to tell you. I can't stand you not being a part of my life, Hannah," Ben said, his voice full of desperation.

Hannah listened, her heart aching for him. She softly replied, "Ben, I can't pretend to know the depth of what you're going through, but I want you to know that you're not alone in this. You have my support, and I believe in you. Confronting your feelings and the difficult truth about your marriage takes immense courage. Nevertheless, I can't deny that it hurt me more than I can say."

Ben took a deep breath and continued, "Thank you, Hannah. Your understanding means more to me than I can express. I can imagine your pain, but please know I've been heartbroken for longer than you could imagine, trapped in the misery of my lonely existence, but talking to you ... it's like finding a lifeline in the storm."

Hannah's voice was filled with uncertainty and empathy as she responded, "I'm not sure how I can stay in your life after finding the truth, but I also cannot leave just like that. I'm sure you're having a hard time, but I hope we can make something worthwhile out of it. I hope we can find the garden beyond the right and wrong…"

The air was simultaneously charged with despair and hope, creating an intense stiffness that seemed to bind them together. The uniqueness of their bond transcended the ordinary and dug into uncharted emotional territory. They were prepared to protect the rare love they felt.

The conversations continued. Every time they hung up the phone, they were highly aware that their journey had only begun, and it was bound to test them in ways they couldn't imagine.

Wild and passionate, their connection was a virtual experience that left them breathless, yearning for more. Although separated by distance, they felt like they could touch each other, an intensity none had ever encountered, a connection that affirmed their destiny—to be together.

Their minds and spirits were inseparable as they lay in their separate beds.

***

Hannah's heart was beating fast. *What would it be like to see him in person?* After the revelation of his marriage, she pondered whether they should remain friends or if it was time to end it for good.

Her heart agreed it was time to move beyond phone calls and messages. Her head was wary, but she had to test their love to see if it was real.

She couldn't bear the thought of not knowing what could have been.

The doubts and fears swirled in Hannah's mind like a raging storm, but as she listened to Ben's voice over the phone, the warmth of his words melted her. "Hannah, please let it be safe in your knowledge that I respect your boundaries; our situation is anything but simple, and you have the absolute right to end this anytime you want," he said, his voice serious. "But, you should also know that I want to see you. I need to know if what we feel is what we have."

Her heart swelled at his words; the yearning, the sincerity in his voice, was driving away her doubts. She took a deep breath and finally relented, agreeing to meet him.

She knew this would be a turning point in their relationship. It could be everything they had dreamed of, or reality might fall short of their expectations …

Only time will tell.

Chapter 5

The Date

Hannah's excitement bubbled over as the day of her date with Ben approached. She couldn't contain her joy. She wanted everything to be perfect for their first meeting. The morning was a flurry of activity as she rushed around her apartment, preparing herself for the crucial occasion.

She let the warm water wash away the lingering nerves. Her skin felt rejuvenated, and she couldn't stop smiling as she imagined the day ahead. She carefully chose her outfit, opting for a flattering dress that made her feel confident and attractive. Her fingers trembled as she fastened the delicate necklace, a gift from her grandmother that held sentimental value.

Her hair was styled in loose waves cascading down her shoulders, and her makeup was subtle but enhancing. As she glanced in the mirror, her reflection brought a smile to her face.

She wondered how Ben might react to her appearance. Though nervous, she knew she was ready.

With one last look in the mirror, Hannah embarked on the road where she yet had to learn about the right exit. Today, she would meet the man who had captured her heart over the phone.

The city had endless possibilities, and Hannah was eager to explore them with or without Ben—Fate would decide.

She couldn't help but feel a little conflicted, though. While she was thrilled to finally meet the man she had grown so close to, she also couldn't shake off concerns about the ongoing COVID-19 pandemic. But as they say, 'Distances break distances!' Who knows …

As she navigated the city's bustling streets, she considered the potential risks of meeting in person. Times were uncertain, but so was life. She appreciated him driving all the way to New York to see her.

She tightened the strap of her mask as her determination to meet Ben overrode all concerns.

***

Her favorite café felt cozier than ever today. Hannah's idea of Ben was better in her imagination as she wasn't a person who would rely on pictures and that, too, on a dating app. Appearances are deceptive, as they say. She would rather meet in person and see the soul through the eyes.

The light breeze teased the silky waves of her shiny, dark hair. She sipped her coffee and put down the mug, and as she looked up, there he was, looking more dashing than she could ever imagine. Light brown, silky hair was complimenting his fair skin. The dark blue eyes seemed to be matching with his shirt. As their eyes met, she knew that reality beat her imagination. Seeing the yellow tulips in his hands was enough to know it was him. *What a fairytale beginning…*

Ben had no difficulty identifying the pretty lady sitting elegantly, sipping her coffee while lost in thoughts. Her smile was constant, as if her thoughts were teasing her. He felt a wave of warmth wash over him.

Ben's gaze was locked on Hannah as he walked towards her table, unable to take his eyes off her. She looked stunning in a sleek black dress that hugged her curves in all the right places. Her hair was in loose waves, and she wore elegant diamond earrings, but their shine dimmed compared to the shine in her eyes. Ben was mesmerized….

Without a word, he handed her a bouquet of yellow tulips. Hannah appeared pleasantly surprised and found herself blushing as she took a gentle whiff of the flowers.

"Hannah?" She melted hearing that voice in person.

"Yes, Ben?"

"No, it's Sean here!" She burst out laughing at the spontaneity. *"A gentleman with a sweet sense of humor. Wouldn't life be great!" she thought.*

"Thank you, they're beautiful," she said, a smile spreading across her face.

"You're welcome," Ben replied, a hint of a smirk on his lips as he looked at her angelic face.

After some time in the cozy café, they walked towards his car. Hannah felt so reassured in his presence. He offered his hand as she took a step on the curb. Their fingers intertwined, and the warmth tickled a feeling she didn't want to let go, they laughed, joked, and got lost in each other's company during the ride and Ben's hand again reached Hannah's.

"I'm glad you said yes," Ben said, looking at Hannah with a charismatic expression.

"I'm glad you came," Hannah replied, feeling content. She couldn't believe being at such ease.

Ben turned on the radio, and John Legend's "All of Me" started playing. It was Hannah's favorite song, but he spoke before she could tell him.

"This song is my all-time favorite. I can't help but dance to it each time I hear it."

Hannah chuckled, "No way, it tops my playlist!"

"Well, that's chemistry. Do you want to get out of the car?" Ben asked enthusiastically.

They pulled up on the side of the road, and Ben turned up the volume. They went into an empty alley and danced to their favorite song.

Hannah hadn't felt this electricity in a long time. Ben was ecstatic seeing her so happy, his nerves relaxed.

They swayed, dancing their hearts out as John Legend's 'All of Me' song was playing in the background. This was an out-of-body experience unlike the anticipated. Love has the power to bring back the child in you who wants to break free and dance around in unbarred pleasure.

Ben started singing along, and Hannah joined in. The way their bodies moved together was so graceful, as if they had been dancing together for years. It was almost like muscle memory. And then, the song came to a close, and something shifted between them.

The lyrics struck a chord, and they felt ... love. Time seemed to stand still, leaving them the only two people in the world. With the streets utterly deserted, the feeling was all the more fitting.

The eyes met, and everything else faded away. Nothing else mattered.

"Ben, this is incredible. I can't believe this is happening," Hannah confessed with a grin.

"Me neither, Hannah. You make everything so much better," Ben replied, his voice laced with emotion. He leaned and kissed her forehead. Hannah blushed with emotion. As he pulled back, Ben recognized the approval in Hannah's eyes; a tender kiss was in order.

Their lips locked, perfectly aligning like puzzle pieces finding their rightful place. In that moment, a rush of passion, long absent from Hannah's life, surged through her. With a blend of tenderness and confidence, Ben kissed her, mindful of the elegant handling Hannah deserved.

As they pulled away, their eyes silently shared a moment of euphoria, a force that transcended the physical world.

Hannah couldn't help but smile as she looked into Ben's eyes. She felt a sense of approval and admiration, which only fueled the burning desire in her.

Ben drew close again, his lips brushing against Hannah's in a gentle embrace, embodying profound respect and deep love.

Their kiss unfolded a story of newfound thirst; their lips melded seamlessly, crafting a moment of perfect harmony that would be etched into their hearts and minds forever. It was a memory that held the promise of a truly extraordinary love

Chapter 6

All of Me

It was time for Ben to drop Hannah back at her place. It was an unusual pain of separation that both equally felt. Holding hands, they walked to the car, silently acknowledging the fleeting nature of their time together. None wanted the night to end, but as all good things come to an end, so did this night of perfection. The drive was comfortably silent, punctuated by the emotion-filled glances they gave each other.

As they pulled up to her apartment building, Hannah turned to face Ben and looked into his eyes. A knot formed in her stomach as she realized this might be the last time. Ben intuitively sensed her apprehension and reached out to kiss her hand.

"Tonight has been amazing, Hannah. I had a wonderful time with you," he said, staring intensely into her eyes, asking and reassuring at the same time.

Hannah nodded, her heart pounding in her chest. "Me too, Ben. I never thought I'd have so much fun in a lockdown."

They shared a light chuckle.

They silently entered Hannah's building and sat for a moment on one of the benches in the lobby, neither wanting to break the spell. Finally, Ben did.

"I know you might be tense about the dynamics of our relationship, Hannah, but I feel like there's something special between us. I would love to see you again if you would. I'll understand if you're not comfortable."

Hannah's heart leaped at the quest. She knew this was a turning point and that whatever answer she gave would determine their future together.

"Yes, Ben. I would very much like to see you again," she said, her voice barely a whisper.

Ben smiled; relief was evident in his eyes. "Good. I'll call you tomorrow then, and we can figure out what we want to do."

They said their goodbyes, and Hannah watched Ben leave with a bittersweet feeling in the pit of her stomach.

When this night started, Hannah had no clue she would feel so strongly for a man she had never met. She knew she was falling for him but also knew the road ahead would be long and bumpy.

Ben took the exit to his house, perplexed about the incredible night he had just experienced. The radio in the car had John Legend's "All of Me" playing. *How uncanny!* He was in utter amazement.

Dumbfounded at the coincidence, he wondered, '*Was it a sign from the universe that this amazing woman was meant to be in his life?*'

He couldn't shake the feeling that she had already changed his life forever and knew he had to see her again.

He also knew that there were obstacles ahead—he was a married man with two daughters.

The mere thought of seeing her again filled him with a fiery passion.

Did she feel the same? *He had to find out.*

Chapter 7

The Argument

Sleep was far away from Ben's eyes. The haunting melody of "All of Me" hung in the air, a poignant reminder of the electrifying connection he shared with Hannah. It was a tune that seemed to carry a message, a cosmic sign pushing him towards an uncharted path, one entwined with Hannah's presence.

The weight of his marital vows suddenly pressed heavily on his conscience, a relentless reminder of the responsibilities and promises made. Torn between the life he had known and the one he wanted, a passion was simmering to be cooked.

The night was shrouded in silence, and the stars shimmered like celestial witnesses to his internal struggle. Ben gazed at the vast expanse of the night sky, searching for answers, a sign, anything to guide him. But the cosmos remained steadfastly still, offering no direction.

Hannah's smile and the touch of her hands kept reverberating through Ben's head. He knew he had to make a choice that would entirely alter his life. The fear of losing everything he held dear tore him apart, but he could also not let go of a love that finally fulfilled him.

As he retired for the day, the world's weight settled upon his shoulders, contemplating the risks and rewards ahead.

Tomorrow, he would talk to Hannah. It was a leap of faith, an act that defied the confines of his familiar world. The uncertainty consumed him with excitement and trepidation, but he couldn't deny the pull, the magnetic force that had drawn them together.

And so, in the stillness of the night, Ben surrendered to the chaos of his feelings, knowing that the dawn would bring the light.

***

As an only child, Ben had grown up in a tumultuous environment, plagued by the emotional abuse of his mother. She blamed him for her continual return to a dead marriage. Whenever she left his father, she threatened to evacuate from his life altogether, tearing him away from friends, school, and the stability he desperately craved. It was a cycle of instability that had left deep scars on his soul.

He had never anticipated falling so profoundly for anyone or expected that connection would shake the very foundation of his existence.

The marriage, COVID, the distances, but fate, it seemed, had other plans in store.

In the confines of his troubled marriage, Ben had imposed upon himself years of sacrifice for the sake of his daughters.

He didn't want them to experience the pain of separation that had scarred his childhood.

Ben's marriage with Sarah had not always been as problematic. They met at a mutual friend's wedding and fell in love. However, the love started to turn bitter shortly after they married. Ben had a sensitive and calm persona, whereas Sarah was possessive and preferred to control everything. As they faced their personalities clash, their communication became a series of heated arguments and silent treatments. Ben craved a deeper emotional connection and instead felt neglected. On the other hand, Sarah found Ben's constant pursuit of passion unsettling, wanting dominance over their lives.

People around them soon started noticing the change in their energy and witnessed the unraveling of their once-promising union. Dinner parties became tense affairs, with forced smiles and whispered arguments in the kitchen.

The birth of their daughters did not bring about much change, except for the fact that both had doted on them and were staying in the loveless marriage only for the sake of the two tiny souls.

Ben found it hard to cope with; separation meant not seeing Emma and Lily every day, something he could not imagine. He could not stand the thought of being separated from them. The constant push and pull between Sarah and Ben made him stoic. He started to distance himself from her and buried himself in work, trying to ensure his calculated schedule would never let his thoughts wander off to the wrong places.

Returning to a life devoid of love felt like a descent from heaven back to earth, a haunting prospect that left him torn between love and the duty of keeping the family together.

***

Ben and Hannah faced their dilemmas, unable to talk openly about their emotions. They ached for each other, but their desires conflicted with their beliefs, perspectives, circumstances, plans, and the societal image they upheld.

Ben's conscience, weighed down by guilt, contended with the harsh criticism from his social circle. Being judged for leaving his daughters behind thickened the uncertainty within him, keeping him trapped in the marriage.

***

One evening, Sarah sat Ben down, her gaze intense, a storm of spite brewing in her eyes. She cast a fleeting look towards their daughters, engrossed in toys in the room's corner, oblivious to the tension that hung between their parents like a dark cloud.

"Ben," Sarah began, her voice laced with an unfamiliar firmness. "We need to talk."

Ben, ever the patient listener, looked at her with a hint of resignation. All this time, he had grown accustomed to these conversations.

Sarah continued, her words sharp and pointed, "I've noticed how you've been distant lately. You think I don't see it, but know that I do. You're always busy with work or your friends, never spending time with us. You're neglecting your family, Ben."

Ben couldn't help but roll his eyes internally, fully aware of the game she was playing. But he stayed silent, letting her continue.

"I want you to know, Ben that our daughters deserve better than this, a father who is present, not some father like figure who is constantly absent. You owe it to them."

Ben sighed, knowing that her words were less about their daughters' well-being and more about her desire to keep him tethered to this loveless marriage. As much as he loved his daughters, the child card, played way too many times, was beginning to take its toll.

Sarah's voice sharpened, slicing through the air. "Listen, Ben," she announced, "You might not love me; believe me, the feeling is mutual. But leaving? That's not an option. I'll make sure of it. Your happiness elsewhere is not my concern, as you're stuck here with us."

At that moment, Ben's eyes opened to the stark reality. It wasn't about love or the semblance of a marriage for Sarah. It was a game of dominance, control, a strategy to keep him under her control. She disgusted him.

With a deep breath, Ben replied, "Sarah, I'll be a responsible father to our daughters. But this isn't fair to either of us. We both deserve happiness, even if it means going our separate ways."

Sarah's expression hardened, her grip on him tightening. She knew she was losing her hold on him, which terrified her. She was willing to do whatever it took to keep him captive in their relationship. Ready to go to lengths, Sarah used manipulation, playing the blame game she was so good at.

But Ben's nature ran deeper, shaped by his past experiences. He had grown up with a bossy, authoritative mother, a woman whose love for his father had made her incapable of severing the ties that bound them.

In contrast, his father had been detached, seeking solace and companionship in the arms of other women. Ben had become an unwitting witness to their dysfunctional dynamic, bearing the brunt of his mother's emotional turmoil. It had left him blemished by guilt, afraid to inflict similar pain upon his wife.

Ben had become a more reclusive person. He started keeping a lot to himself and built a good reputation for the people around him. He had grown to be a follower of rules. He did not deviate from the norms, resulting in a structured and calculated lifestyle. His peers respected him for his image and conformity. It became a significant part of his mundane routine; he did not ever want this image to break down in front of people. Beneath the exterior, he was a vulnerable individual who longed for a satisfying relationship and profound love ... Ben had been doing a great job hiding his weak side until he met Hannah, who brought it out of him. Hannah got the dead man to life, and he felt the courage, after years of compromise, to fight for a life of love.

He was enchanted by her mere existence and wanted to be with her.

Ben contemplated the tough decision, and his heart raced with anticipation. He knew he had to confront the truth, to lay bare his emotions and desires. The time had come to call Hannah, confess, and share the burden of his surreptitious torment.

Taking a deep breath, Ben reached for the phone, his fingers trembling with excitement and apprehension.

The suspense was tightening like a taut wire around his heart. The line rang, the seconds stretching into eternity until finally, a soft voice answered on the other end. "Hello."

"Hannah," Ben began, his voice betraying the emotion that surged within him. "There is something I must tell you, something I can no longer keep buried; about us, about what the future holds for the two of us..."

At that moment, the world seemed to hold its breath as if aware of the seismic shift that was about to occur.

The declaration that would alter their lives forever was made, a confession that would test the limits of their love and challenge the boundaries of their existence.

Ben pressed the phone to his ear while a symphony of emotions danced in his eyes, a silent prelude to the confession he was about to unleash. His voice trembled with every word.

"I love you, Hannah."

There was a long, soothing pause at both ends …

"From the moment our paths crossed, I knew that my heart was forever yours. I have fought against the tide but can no longer hide the truth. You are the missing piece of my soul; will you complete me?"

His words, each syllable, carried the weight of a thousand unsaid words, unraveling the tapestry of their entangled souls.

The silence was deafening. They could hear the sound of their breaths.

Hannah's voice, soft and fragile, broke the stillness.

"Ben ... I love you, too," she whispered, her voice laced with hope and fear. "But how will we navigate our complex situation? Your marriage, responsibilities ... I fear losing you, but I cannot deny the intensity of our connection."

Ben's heart sank at the tremor in her voice, threatening to drown their love in a sea of obligations. But he couldn't put her life on hold while he sought his happiness.

"I want to be with you, Hannah," he said, his voice filled with anguish. "But I cannot ask you to wait for years. It is selfish and disrespectful of your desires and dreams. I have a plan, a timeline to free myself from this suffocating marriage. In five years, when my older daughter leaves for university and the second goes to boarding school, I can leave without feeling like I've abandoned my responsibilities as a father."

Hannah's breath quivered, a stark echo of their grim reality. Their love, once a blazing flame, now flickered under the oppressive weight of circumstance. Their hearts were filled with uncertainty as doubt seeped in.

"It will be hard, Ben. How will I cope in these five years?" she said, her voice fragile. "I'm scared of losing you, but at the same time, I'm scared that your daughters will look at me questionably one day. Wouldn't facing the storm and telling them the truth be better? Perhaps they will understand?" she said, her words filled with sadness.

"I cannot deny the depth of my love for you, how you've awakened parts of me I never knew existed. I want to be with you too, Ben, but the uncertainty and the waiting don't make sense; it feels like I'm drowning."

Ben's heart ached at her words, his love for her only intensifying with each passing moment. He understood the gravity of their predicament. It was a battle between their hearts and minds.

Ben's eyes brimmed with unshed tears in his clinic as he mustered the courage to ask the question that could change their lives.

"Hannah, my dear, I would love to see you again…" It was more of a question than a statement.

In that suspended moment, their hearts beat in synchrony. The answer held the power to shape their future and defy the obstacles.

Finally, Hannah's voice, soft but persistent, broke the silence. "Yes, Ben," she replied, her words carrying the weight of their shared desires. "Come to my apartment since all the venues are in lockdown; I'm sure we can work this out." The call ended, and a sense of euphoria washed over Ben. The world around them was a blur, but he had to enter the unknown and face the consequences for the sake of their hearts.

***

The COVID lockdown had enveloped the United States beyond anticipation.

The world outside had reached a standstill, and Ben felt trapped within his home in New Jersey. The once bustling streets now echoed an eerie silence as if the very pulse of life had come to a standstill.

The short distance between them seemed to have grown insurmountable, aggravated by the barriers imposed by the lockdown. The congested streets now resembled remote islands. , rendering their desires for physical proximity an impossible reverie.

In the depths of their hearts, Ben and Hannah's connection, initially kindled during their heartfelt conversations, now blazed brightly. But despite the zeal, the circumstances appeared to conspire against their union. The lockdown, a relentless and unyielding antagonist, cast shadows of frustration.

Weeks stretched into months, but their painful separation persisted. COVID seemed to have a mission, a poignant reminder for people not to take precious moments for granted and cherish them before they go missing—the days filled with thoughts of what could have brought the taste of unfulfilled longings—bitterly sweet.

Arguments punctuated conversations. Each disagreement only magnified the underlying tension, a relentless reminder of human connection.

Hannah needed him, and Ben was burdened by his inability to be there for her. With imposed isolation, he was forced to confront the magnitude of his feelings and the consequences ahead.

As they grappled with the unbearable helplessness every day, Ben and Hannah grew more aware of the stakes involved. Their love became a force that demanded resolution, urging them to face their demons and make choices that would shape their futures. However, the ball was in Ben's court, but his daughters bound his judgment. Like a pressure cooker, the confines of the lockdown heightened the intensity of their emotions like so many others and pushed them to the brink.

Hannah's fears got the best of her as she wished for better control over the situation. Despite her yearning for him, she struggled not to give Ben too much access to her heart. She had to be sure. She had to protect her heart and dignity all the same.

The lockdown—a metaphorical prison, teased them with glimpses of what could be but withheld the fulfillment they desperately sought. They had no choice but to wait.

***

Two months had passed since their first meeting, yet the bond grew stronger.

In the wake of a long, dark lockdown period, a bright ray of hope pierced, the restrictions were lifted! This news sparked a thrilling jolt in Ben's heart as he eagerly but nervously prepared for a quest he'd long awaited. With his heart pounding with excitement, he set off on a journey that felt like a lifetime.

As he drove towards Hannah's place, a perfect reflection of the storm inside him made every beat of the pulse feel the promise of a joyous beginning.

Arriving at her doorstep, Ben's knock on the door echoed through the quiet neighborhood, a gentle but persistent sound that heralded his presence. Hannah opened the door, an electric, unspoken recognition of the time lost and the burning desire speaking in their eyes. Time stopped.

Without a word, Hannah took him in her warm embrace; their bodies moved as if following an intricate, passionate dance choreographed by heart's desire. Their kiss was a fierce declaration of love, a physical manifestation of all the words they had exchanged during the weeks of separation. In that magical moment, COVID was the last thing on their minds; their bodies, entwined in perfect harmony, became a testament to the profound depth of a bond that knew no boundaries.

Were they dreaming?

Even if it was, the dream continued with light banter and joyful smiles with no need for complaints. With a promise to meet for breakfast, Ben kissed her goodbye. Hannah, who knew the art of playing with words, found no urge to speak. She waved goodbye to him with sparkles in her eyes.

***

The morning light streaming through the window at Hannah's dining table never seemed so bright.

Their conversation was gentle, but Ben's presence had all Hannah needed. After a while, their emotions began to surface.

Hannah finally gathered the courage to say, "Ben," she began, trembling, "I need to know you're willing to fight for us. I've been hurt before, but there's something about us; I've let you into my heart and life, and I need to feel I'm more than just another chapter in your story."

Ben's expression softened. He took her hand and pressed gently, understanding her genuine concern. "Hannah, you are special to me, more than I can say. I know I haven't been open before. But it's not for lack of wanting to, but some things clouded my judgment, things I can't just cast aside."

Hannah nodded, her gaze fixed on him. "Is it your daughters or something else that's keeping you?" she asked, her voice had a tinge of frustration. "I know they're important, but it feels like they cast a long shadow over what we have."

Ben sighed, running a hand through his hair. "Yes, it's my daughters. My marriage to Sarah has become a comfortable cocoon for them, even though it's loveless. I can't just break free from that without causing them immense pain. Hannah, I can't begin to describe what it is like … a father's heart … it makes you almost a coward."

Hannah's eyes filled with empathy. "I get that, Ben. I do. But what about us? I want a future with you. How can I stand by you if you keep me in the shadow, in a secret relationship?"

Ben looked down, struggling to find the right words. "Hannah, it's not about keeping you hidden. It's about the complexity of my situation. I need time to figure it out, but I can't lose you."

Tears welled in Hannah's eyes as she responded, "I want to believe you, Ben. But every time you hesitate or pull back, it shatters my trust. I need to know that we're in this together."

Ben reached across the table and hugged Hannah so gently that she felt she would melt. "I'm willing to fight, Hannah. I promise," he whispered in her ear. "But I can't promise a quick fix. I hope you'll be patient for us; I won't let you down."

Hannah just looked at him, her gaze a mix of relief and grit. "I'll be patient, Ben, because I believe in what we have. Just don't make me wait forever."

'His divorce carried the risk his daughters would resent him and might even never want to meet him again if they found out about his decision to leave their mother to be with another woman. He would have to learn to live without them.' Even the thought terrified him; he wasn't ready for it, but he knew he couldn't lose Hannah and would have to figure it out sooner rather than later.

Ben and Hannah glanced at the phone, curiosity giving way to concern as they saw it was his wife, Sarah.

Ben hesitated for a moment; it had been hardly 24 hours since he left the house to be with Hannah finally, but now it appeared that a stark reminder of the life he was entangled in, had come to disrupt the long-awaited peace.

Timidly, he answered, and the tension in the room excavated as he listened to the urgency in Sarah's voice. It was every parent's worst fear — their daughter had been in an accident at school and had broken her arm. She had been rushed to the hospital, and Sarah was frantically trying to reach Ben, her voice shaking with distress.

Ben's face turned ashen as he absorbed the news. His mind raced, torn between the two worlds that had suddenly collided. He had taken this precious time to be with Hannah, to strengthen their connection, and now he was faced with a family crisis that demanded his immediate attention.

On a business trip in Washington, Sarah had no choice but to call Ben, as she couldn't be there for their daughter. He assured her he would be at the hospital as quickly as possible (which meant leaving immediately).

Turning to Hannah, his face etched with regret, he spoke, his voice heavy, "I'm sorry, Hannah. It's my daughter. She's had an accident ….."

Hannah put her hand on his mouth. "Shhh… go, Ben, we'll talk later, okay?" she said softly, touching his arm. "Drive safe. We'll find a way through this."

With tears in his eyes, Ben kissed her passionately, caressed her cheek, and left; their precious time together was cut short by the stark knock of reality. As he rushed to be by his daughter's side, he couldn't help but feel the weight of his choices and their impact on the people he cared about. He felt his heart was hit with a sledgehammer.

***

The journey back to New Jersey and the hospital was agonizing, his thoughts a tumultuous whirlwind of self-reproach. He reached the hospital, pushed open the doors, and made his way to her room, determined to put his family first, no matter the complications and complexities that had recently surfaced in his life.

The crossroads he stood at cast an ominous shadow on Ben's heart. The delicate balance between his daughters and Hannah teetered precariously, the weight of his decisions threatening to crush them all.

The divorce he contemplated would mean limited time with his precious daughters, a sacrifice too challenging to bear. Yet, Hannah couldn't be kept in the shadows.

The stage was set for a pivotal moment when the threads of their lives would be woven together or forever unraveled. The stakes were high, the tension unbearable, and the fate of their hearts hung in the balance.

***

The night was heavy with anticipation as Hannah nervously dialed Ben's number, her heart pounding.

She needed answers and reassurance. She felt like life was slipping through her fingers like grains of sand. The phone rang, each chime echoing in the silence of her room until he finally picked up. He sounded detached, and that struck her like a dagger to the heart.

"Ben, it's me," she whispered, her voice trembling with unspoken emotions. "I just wanted to know how your daughter is doing. Is she alright?"

The silence was a void, a heavy pause that felt like time had frozen, waiting for his reaction. When he finally spoke, his words cut through the air, cold and distant, like a sharp wind in a barren land. She felt an acute sense of abandonment, a deep-seated pain that resonated with the emptiness of his response.

"She's fine, Hannah. She's been taken care of," Ben replied quietly.

"Good to know," Hannah whispered, her heart shattering into tiny pieces.

Ben realized the impact of his coldness in Hannah's voice. A wave of regret washed over him. He responded at once with earnestness.

"Hannah, I'm sorry; I never wanted to hurt you or make you feel bad. I'm just so upset and bloody confused… I'm…."

Hannah held her tears back. "Ben, it was tough for me when you left; I felt abandoned even though I understood."

Ben nodded, though Hannah couldn't see him. "Yes, Hannah. I'm sorry; I should have communicated with you. I should have treated you better, and I should have called you."

Hannah hesitated before speaking. "Ben, I need time," she said, her voice filled with determination. "I must separate myself from your obligations and figure out my emotions. I have lived my pain, and I can't live yours any more than you can. I hope you can figure out what is to be done."

Ben, though surprised, appreciated Hannah's ask. "I understand, Hannah," he said softly. "Please take your time, and I'll use mine."

"Thanks, Ben. I hope this time helps us know better what we want."

"I hope so, too, Hannah," Ben said sincerely. "I'll do everything to fix it, hoping not to hurt anyone."

Hannah and Ben knew the implications of their choices as their call ended. The pain was as deep as was the need to reflect.

They knew the path ahead would be grim, but who said it would be easy?

Chapter 8

The Secret

They must've been the two longest weeks of her life since she last spoke with Ben.

The silence between them grew increasingly heavy, each day heavier than the previous. Despite Ben's apology for not answering Hannah's calls on the day of the accident, the gap between them only amplified, exacerbating the pain.

Sarah was aware of the tensions straining their marriage, as she had long sensed something was amiss, and the incident involving their daughter intensified her control over Ben. She became obsessively possessive, monitoring all his actions with mounting suspicion.

Sarah's constant surveillance was suffocating Ben. She seized every opportunity to make him feel guilty. Their daughter's accident, in her mind, was the perfect opportunity to prove to him that he was neglecting his duties as a husband and a father. She used this incident to assert her control and push Ben further into a corner. Although the daughter was in school when she got into the accident, it couldn't be his fault. Nevertheless, Sarah knew the trick!

This constant monitoring and the weight of her guilt-tripping became insufferable for Ben. It tormented his conscience and threatened to unravel the delicate threads holding his life together.

Meanwhile, Hannah had taken the opportunity to step back from the relationship to clear her mind and make important decisions. Lately, she had started feeling like she was losing control over her feelings.

Despite their distance, the last conversation continued to haunt them.

Hannah paced in her apartment, her heart burdened with sadness and anger. Desperately needing a shoulder, she yearned to return to her mother. Hannah had always confided in her, even when she had left her family house to travel around the world for her career. She found great support and empowerment in her, especially when life threw her off balance with challenges.

Her parents' separation had been a nonviolent one, but it had left a lasting impact on her. Her mother was a proud, independent woman from a lineage of wealth and was always an idealist who would never compromise for a man. Her dad was a self-made, successful career person, well-traveled, and wanted to impart his knowledge to his children. Like her mother, an engineer with a strong passion for music, art, and literature, he refined his taste and family heritage.

Hannah grew up with high standards and values that strongly wired her brain and built her character. She got her resilience, positivity, and "can do" attitude from her mom and her intelligence, intellect, and independence from her dad. She was distinguished among her siblings as she always aimed high and never feared any challenge.

Madly in love, Hannah knew she had to be strong and keep her distance; the pandemic certainly made it easier—a blessing in disguise.

On the other side, Ben couldn't stop thinking about Hannah.

His thoughts consumed him. He missed her presence, her infectious laughter, and how she made him feel alive. But he also knew he had let her down, and the thought incessantly badgered him.

The fire was equally burning on both ends, but so was the suffering, each carrying the weight of their pain alone. Ben attempted to divert his attention towards work but to no avail. Hannah was no ordinary woman, and Ben could no longer bear the silence.

He needed to do something.

He decided to send her favorite flowers, yellow tulips, hoping it would bring a smile to her heart—her aching heart.

Would she accept his gesture?

The hesitation was distressing, but he knew he had to try.

***

The morning sun shone through, and she stirred in her sleep, feeling a sense of unease.

It wasn't until she opened her eyes and saw her phone swarming with missed calls and messages from Ben that she realized what was causing it.

Her heart fluttered as she quickly scrolled through the messages. The yellow tulips Ben sent were still sitting on her bedside table, their vibrant petals glowing in the early morning light.

She felt a rush of emotions as she called him back; the desperation in his voice was eminent.

Hannah's voice was tinged with melancholy, "Ben, I had a dream last night ... I saw a cozy house with sunlight streaming through big, open windows. The aroma of freshly brewed coffee lingered in the air, and we were sitting at the kitchen table."

 Softly, he said, "Oh, Hannah, I long for your dream to come true. I imagine us traveling to places, experiencing adventures, and collecting countless memories together. I see us laughing, exploring, and finding solace in each other even when I'm awake."

Grace laced her words, "I long for a love that's not hidden, Ben. A relationship that's celebrated and not kept underground. I can't choose for you, but I can tell you that it is very hard for me to think of us in this situation, where words are deprived of action, and the decision is hindered by vulnerability."

Ben's voice was regretful but filled with affection. "You have no idea how much I want that, Hannah. I'm trying, but it is not easy. The guilt ... it's relentless."

She refrained from tapping the sensitive nerve of his heart for a while, and they continued to chat for a few moments, laughing, flirting, and lost in the gift of the present moment.

Eventually, Ben had to leave her to attend to a patient in his clinic, but he had a fire burning in him, aware of the smoke on the other side, too.

***

The night was quiet, and the stars shone brightly in the sky like diamonds scattered on a black velvet canvas.

Ben and Hannah were on the moon, the endless calls, the chemistry, the laughter as if all the lost years were bliss; the door of the treasured love had to open now. They were lost in their fairytale of love and passion, safe in their knowledge the key was yet to be found.

Hannah felt Ben was keeping something from her. She could sense it in how he sometimes hesitated when discussing certain subjects. But she dared not ask; she couldn't lose the rare moments of their joint laughter.

We shall see… she thought!

But one night, something changed. As they spoke about their hopes and dreams, Ben's voice quivered as he confessed to her a truth he had kept from the world.

As Hannah listened intently, her heart raced with every word he spoke.

Ben had been molested by his school teacher when he was just 12 years old. For two years, the teacher held him hostage to her sexual fantasies until he finally gathered the courage to break free.

Ben had never been able to share the fracturing experience with his mum or dad, and all these years, it had been eating him up. He only shared with his therapist, but now, after ages, Hannah was the one to embrace his pain. Such is the power of love!

But the most significant discovery for Hannah didn't stop at this; it was the aftermath of this sexual abuse that shook her to the core.

Ben had developed masochistic sexual fantasies that he couldn't share with any of his preceding relationships, not even Sarah. He was resisting hard not to fall into these fantasies. Although he tried several times, he failed and felt terrible about his mental struggle.

What horrified him the most was the fear of being judged, labeled, cornered, and unaccepted. Ben, who always portrayed the profile of a strong, successful man, a great leader at work, a wonderful father at home, and a significant influencer in his community, was hiding a deep, dark secret.

He finally had to seek professional help to be able to cope with the trauma; that took a lot of courage to open up to his therapist about his experience and its aftermath—the bizarre sexual fantasies.

He could never muster up the courage to confront the teacher, but after graduating from university, he went back to his school, where she was still teaching. He went to her and brought up what she did to him all those years. Being the dominant and merciless woman that she was, she completely dismissed him and denied flat on his face that she ever did what he implied. He knew no one in the school management would believe him as it had been a long time since the incident, and he didn't have any evidence to prove the teacher's abuse.

Now, he took a considerable risk to share his secret with Hannah, as deep inside, he knew she was the only one in the world who would accept him, all of him, and not judge him. He had never felt so safe nor dared to open up and be as vulnerable as he was.

"Ben," she eventually spoke, compassion dripping from her voice, "Thank you for trusting me with something so personal. I can't imagine your sorrow throughout the years. However, I'm here for you now."

Tears welled up in Ben's eyes as he felt a wave of relief wash over him. Hannah's response was everything he could ideally wish for.

"Hannah, I've struggled with my emotions for a very long time, and the impact it has had on my heart has been devastating, but you are so kind," Ben said. "I feel safe with you. With your support, I can work through this, too, and find the road to healing."

Hannah sounded determined. "Ben, you're more brave than you think. Just know you're not alone in this. We're in this together. I'll walk that road with you until you find the crevice to express your emotions without the burden of guilt. We'll take it one step at a time."

Hannah's empathy and support overwhelmed Ben. He knew opening up to her was the right decision, and he felt light as a feather.

"Thank you, Hannah," he said. "I never knew someone like you existed. I'm forever grateful."

Hannah's voice reassured, "Ben, you're not your history or an Algebra problem. You'll overcome this and be stronger. I will always be here."

As the weight of their shared truth sank in, Ben and Hannah knew they had taken the first step forward. To be loved is a gift, to be embraced with your pain is a blessing…

Hannah felt compassion for him as she tried to absorb the depth of his pain. The magnitude of the discovery overwhelmed her.

In all those times of togetherness, they had never felt as close as they did in that moment.

As they said their goodbyes, Hannah knew she was dealing with the kind of love trapped in deep wounds.

After learning about Ben's secret, she felt they were bound. She would have to navigate the waters of love with an emotionally wounded, married man. And yet, she was willing and gratified to bask in its glory and warmth. It was a territory unknown to her.

Chapter 9

A Beautiful Day

The pandemic, like a dark overture, echoed through the empty boulevards. Doors remained closed, windows veiled, and people sought shelter in the solitude of their dwellings. Isolation and desolation became steadfast companions, and the absence of the tender embrace of family and friends left hearts heavy with longing.

Days melted into weeks, and the once-familiar routines lost their advantages, becoming a vague, formless haze. Emotions tumbled and swirled, melancholy soaking the spirit with an unquenchable yearning. The human spirit was tested, as the pandemic's grip seemed unyielding, but a glimmer of hope emerged in the depths of this collective darkness.

After five weeks, Ben and Hannah were meeting again today.

Ben navigated the bureaucratic maze tenaciously, ensuring a long-anticipated reunion with his beloved.

As their eyes met, it was a moment suspended in time of a much-longed-for reunion. Hannah surged into his waiting arms, a deluge of emotions cascading down her cheeks and her soul quivering with anticipation. Ben's touch was tender and respectful, his lips planting soft kisses upon her forehead.

A night of enchantment unfurled under the gentle moon's illumination, weaving a tapestry of magic around them. The embrace of his arms, a sanctuary, where her burdens melted into the obscurity of the night.

Their conversation meandered with a natural rhythm throughout the night, their words like stars scattered across the infinite cosmos, illuminating the uncharted territory of their subterranean chemistry.

The minutes slipped unnoticed as their love transcended the confines of time. The serene experience made their hearts dance in graceful harmony, embracing the gentle cadence of esprit de corps.

"I have something for you," whispered Ben, his fingers tracing a tender path along the inside of her wrist.

"What?" asked Hannah, a smile playing on her lips.

With a gentle flourish, Ben retrieved a small velvet box from his pocket, delicately tracing the fabric with his fingertips. As he opened the box, Hannah's eyes expanded, captivated by the sight that unfolded before her—a beautiful diamond bracelet with its elegant craftsmanship glistening in the light.

"It's beautiful, Ben," she whispered as he clasped the bracelet around her wrist and hugged him.

Fate, the whimsical master of illusions, relished its artful gamesmanship. Ben and Hannah shared the magical night, absorbed in each other's arms. Their favorite song set the tone, creating a dreamy ambiance. Dancing, they connected on a deeper emotive level, their intimacy evolving beyond the physical.

As the night unfolded, Ben and Hannah found renewed purpose as they let the sad melodies disappear.

As the first light of dawn tiptoed into the room, delicate sunbeams streamed through the parted curtains, painting a golden embroidery on the floor, like a silent tribute to the slumbering figures—Hannah and Ben.

***

Hannah, cradled in the cocoon of her dreams, began to stir. The gentle warmth of the sun's embrace graced her face, coaxing her back to consciousness. Across the room, Ben, having awakened from his peaceful slumber on the couch, found himself irresistibly drawn to the sight of her bathed in the morning's soft glow. A tender smile graced his lips as he approached her, his steps as light as whispers, careful not to disrupt the serenity.

Gently, he bent down and kissed her forehead. In the loving gesture, he expressed all the unspoken words that had taken root between them.

"Darling," he whispered against her lips, the weight of his impending departure evident in his voice. His words carried a bittersweet melody tinged with the sorrow of separation.

After a brief pause, Hannah mustered her courage and spoke softly, her words laced with hope, "You don't have to go, you know."

Ben's eyes sparkled as he gently broke away from her embrace. "And yet, I must," he said, his voice resigning, but he managed to smile for her. "And you know why."

Hannah rose, gently turning Ben to face her. "Do you love me, Ben?" she asked, her voice sad.

With a sad smile, Ben responded, "Can you doubt it?"

"Then," said Hannah, taking his hands in hers. "Stay. Please. I cannot bear the distance anymore. We can … we can figure this out. We will make it work. I know we can. You have to believe in me, in us."

A moment of poignant silence passed between them as Ben looked away, his heart torn between the present's desires and the future's qualms. "I will," he whispered, "But we must wait for the right time."

And with that, he slipped away, leaving Hannah with a gale of unresolved emotions.

***

In the storm of sentiments, her thoughts scattered like shards from a shattered mirror, reflecting her heart's feelings. What was their love? She wondered. Was it an ethereal facade, an illusion, or a fleeting dream? Did he hold her in the same regard she did, or were his affections transitory conquests, captivating but momentary? The weight of these unanswered questions pressed against her spirit, a burden she could hardly bear.

Why didn't he fight for their love? Were there warning signs she had been blind to, or was she guilty of investing too much faith in their bond? The unyielding, untouchable nature of their situation baffled her. *Were his daughters the sole reason, or was something else concealed beneath the surface?*

His words, his constant expressions of anguish at the mere thought of her vanishing from his life, echoed endlessly in her mind. Was his pain powerful? And if so, why was he paralyzed, unable to take action or make a choice? *Could he let her go without a fight?*

Caught in the whirlpool of thoughts and assumptions, she could no longer carry the baggage. Her life had become a relentless struggle, a facade of composure.

Alone in her dimly lit living room, Hannah mulled over a decision spurred by growing unrest. Clutching her phone, she scrolled past messages, seeking answers to the mystery Ben had concealed about his family. The recent encounters and unexplained absences had fueled a sense of ambiguity that she could no longer ignore.

After much contemplation, she mustered the resolve to reach out to him, asking to meet one last time. She needed to know, once and for all, whether they were ever meant to be.

Chapter 10

The Battle of Heart

Hannah's pulse raced as she sat in her living room, making her rethink everything.

In her despair, Hannah realized that she had overlooked the glaring red flags in her relationship. Recalling Ben's distant gaze and preoccupied mind, she questioned how these signs had eluded her.

Doubts swirled through her mind like a cyclone. She deliberated if she was just another notch in Ben's belt— exploited and discarded.

On the other hand, Ben's marriage now seemed an insurmountable barrier, deepening their predicament. The presence of his daughters constantly reminded them of the boundaries they dared not cross. Hannah, wrapped in a cloak of melancholy and desire, questioned whether their love was doomed from the start—destined to remain unfulfilled.

Hannah's assumptions clashed as she struggled with pain and perplexity. She relived every memory in her mind for explanations she couldn't fathom. Her job and social life were also affected.

Hannah, in a constant state of anxiety, started skipping meals and neglecting the needs that she once prioritized. She began to withdraw socially, her usual charm and enthusiasm fading. She avoided going out and even missed a few deadlines. Her life was no longer calculated; her discipline flew out of the window where love had entered.

As her closest friend, Cara tried uplifting Hannah's mood over lunch one day at a café she loved. "I've noticed you haven't been taking care of yourself, hon. You seem to be somewhere else, even in meetings," she said with concern. "Is there something you want to tell me about? Something weighing you down? You know I'm here for you, right?"

"I know, Cara," said Hannah. "But I don't think talking about it will fix anything."

"Why do you think it won't, Hannah?"

"It just won't; you won't get it," Hannah said, on the verge of tears.

"Hannah, I know it might seem like there's no way out, but I want you to know that sharing your burden will make you feel better. You don't have to do this alone; I'm here for you."

"It's hard to say, Cara; I fail to see how any of this is ever going to work out," said Hannah, praying the conversation would die down as she did not want to even think about it.

As the days passed, Hannah's battle grew intolerable, like an unseen weight on her shoulders. She longed for freedom, a chance to face Ben and get all the answers.

Hannah informed him via text about her soul-wrenching thoughts. To reconcile her vision of their love, she shared her hammering feelings and the harsh reality that had encircled her.

Hannah's heart pounded as she pressed the 'enter' button, her breath held in suspense. Fear of the unknown gripped her, yet she knew she couldn't hide from it. Hence, she dispatched a message into the digital abyss. Lingering in a delicate balance of hope and despair, she eagerly anticipated his response.

***

Ben was surrounded by laughter and banter with his guests in his home. However, Hannah continued to dominate his thoughts. The weight of their relationship pressed upon his heart, and he couldn't shake the feeling of impending doom.

His phone rang, snapping him out of his trance. Seeing Hannah's name on the screen, he opened the message hesitantly.

Hannah: *Ben, I'm emotionally drained, questioning our love. Why didn't you fight for us? The pain is overwhelming; I trusted you, but now I'm unsure. Has our love failed, or is it a puzzle you've moved on from? Our relationship feels buried, eroding our connection. I need answers and honesty. I can't wait for forever. Must we go our separate ways? Our journey isn't as I imagined, but life is unpredictable. I'll cherish our love, but it's time to part ways. Please come and meet me if you have better answers.*

As he read her words, Ben's heart sank. A cyclone passed through his core, leaving only devastation. Hannah, the joyful, strong, cheerful lady, surprised him with her sadness.

Guilt took the best of him. How could he have allowed this? How could he have failed her?

After realizing the extent of his blunders, Ben began to question his motives, judgments, and outcomes. His worst misgivings now plagued his every thought.

The enormous conflict in his soul masked the clamor of the gathering around him. He excused himself and left his guests in awe.

Ben wandered the city streets, thinking about her. The roads seemed empty and chilly. He walked between his gloomy thoughts and self-blame. How could he have been so oblivious to the consequences of his actions? How could he have let their love slip through his fingers?

With rain pouring down on his cheeks, each droplet felt like a mirror of his inner mayhem. He sought solace in the city's grandeur, yet its magnificence only reverberated his grief.

Ben arrived at a park after hours and slumped on a bench. In the stillness of the night, regret overwhelmed him like a tide. He wished he could change the climax of their love tale. But he knew the time had only marched ahead.

Ben's thoughts and misery carried along with the night, nearly overcome by the realization of what he stood to lose.

In his despair, a resolve emerged.

Ben wiped his eyes and got up from the bench. He returned home with a newfound purpose. *The wounds are meant to be healed when bandaged with love. If left open in cold air, they hurt.*

A feeling of prudence permeated the night. Ben approached his house with renewed sanguinity, not knowing of the unexpected turn of events.

Meanwhile, the lockdown restrictions began to soften. However, the universe seemed to have heard his quiet appeal, allowing him to bridge the killer gap. He had decided, and the heart wouldn't resist this time.

Ben's heart raced, knowing reconciliation would be difficult, but he was determined to fight to the finish. He had to; it was no ordinary batter—the battle of heart. He made the early morning plan.

Restlessness and anticipation lasted all night, but hope blazed stronger in his chest.

Chapter 11

Goodbye

Ben drove to Hannah's house as the sun rose over the city, providing a golden light. New York was waiting…

After the restive night, his eyes strained to concentrate at 7 am. He felt her radiating through his thoughts, pulling him towards her like a magnetic force. Traffic, landscape, and everything else didn't matter. Only his intense longing to be with her existed.

Time was crawling as he raced towards his destination.

With each mile, his determination strengthened, and his promise reinforced, even if it meant addressing his issues and making hard choices. *He will fight for their love, come what may.*

He arrived at her door at last. As he got out of the car with anticipation and apprehension, Hannah appeared at the door, her eyes happy and sad all at once.

Without a word, they embraced, their arms wrapping around each other tightly like two magnets. It was the longest, warmest, and saddest hug ever, conveying harsh reality's pain and barbs.

Hannah cried in his arms. Her emotions spilled the weight of their separation. Ben pressed Hannah's against his chest. Hannah's distress pierced his spirit, further strengthening his resolve. He hugged her passionately and repeatedly, expressing that he understood her anguish and was there for her.

It was time for catharsis.

After moments of silent exchanges, Hannah spoke, her voice a symphony of pain, desire, love, and hope. "Ben, I've missed you so much," she cried. "I miss you every day. It breaks my heart."

Ben's voice was soft, his grip tight. "Hannah, I miss you, too. You're my world; being without you is like missing the earth underneath my feet."

Hannah buried her face in his chest, his shirt embracing her tears. "Ben, I cannot bring myself to let you go, but I cannot dwell in this limbo. It's too painful not to be in your life every day. I dreamt to be someone's priority, not the option, just as your girls are yours."

Ben's voice broke with agony. "You're not an option to me, Hannah. Circumstances have placed us in this predicament. But I understand your feelings and don't want to hold you back. You deserve the best, and I can't watch you struggle because of me."

"We can't carry on like this, Ben," she began, her voice barely above a whisper. "I'm torn between my love for you and the pain of not having you. The thought of being the cause of turmoil in your family tears me apart. I don't want to be the reason for anyone's hurt, especially not yours or your daughters'."

Her trembling hands clenched into fists, trying to contain the overwhelming feelings.

"I'm in much pain, Ben, and I can't bear it any longer. It's like a constant ache in my heart, and I can't take it," she continued, her tears falling freely. "Maybe we should call it off, let go of what we have. If we're truly meant to be together, fate will find a way to reunite us someday."

The pain in her eyes mirrored the pain in his heart, and Ben could feel his world crumbling around him. He reached out to comfort her, but his touch felt empty, unable to mend the rift that was tearing them apart.

"I don't want to lose you, Hannah," he whispered, his voice choked with emotion. "But I can't bear to see you suffer because of me. You deserve more than this half-hearted love, and I can't forgive myself for putting you through this. Hannah, I can't deny your pain; I know you're hurting. I love you too much to see you in this state," he said softly, his voice cracking with emotion. "But I don't want you to think you're a burden to me. You're not. I want to be there for you, to support you through every challenge. I want to be the one you lean on when life gets tough."

His grip on her hands tightened as he continued, "I know you're going through a difficult time, and it's tearing me apart that I can't take away your pain. But please understand that your happiness is not dependent on me. I want you to prioritize yourself and find the happiness you deserve, even if it means being apart."

His eyes were filled with sadness as he spoke his truth, "You're right in thinking your pain is bigger than mine, and I don't want to add to it. But please, don't think you're being selfish for expressing what you feel. It's essential to do so, and if that means distance, then I'll respect your decision."

The weight of their parting left the room silent. Hannah recognized that she couldn't put her life on hold while waiting for the unknown. She couldn't sacrifice her self-worth by settling for a shadowy presence.

It was a wordless exchange of anguish, misery, and loss between two souls. Each minute ticking away brought Ben closer to departure, turning the space into a sanctuary of their shared sorrow. The heaviness of impending farewell swung in the air.

They clutched each other—their chests ached with the painful goodbye.

The night progressed as they slept, holding each other.

***

Ben softly got out of bed and went to the kitchen. He knew her daily routine and adored making her breakfast. He poured her favorite coffee, meticulously arranged a fruit salad with crunchy almonds, and went to the bakery next door to get her favorite muffins.

After returning, Ben put the tray on the bedside table and softly kissed Hannah's forehead to wake her up. His kindness made her grin. With a loving look in his eyes, he snuggled back into her arms

The breakfast in bed was divine. As Ben gently fed her, Hannah ate like a princess. She fell in love again! The moment was Blissful.

After breakfast, Ben grabbed her hand and brought her to the living room, where he had prepared a surprise. Hannah's eyes brightened as he played her favorite playlist, and she couldn't help but sway. Her beautiful motions in her silky, flowing evening gown melted his heart.

The dance was a perfect synchronization of their love. They dived deeper into their magical bubble as the world faded away. In that moment, it felt like a love that transcended everything.

They swayed to the music and smiled at the lyrics, knowing well that their time together was diminishing; they wanted to cherish it like a forever memory, safe in their hearts.

The imminent parting was coming closer as the hours they had left together dwindled. Ben had to go….

They reluctantly relinquished their grasp—a painful goodbye—a wordless wave.

Hannah watched him go, knowing their lives were about to diverge. She ran the distance and covered his lips with hers.

The parting kiss—time seemed to stand still. Their bodies squeezed together as though seeking to merge, their hearts beating as one.

Life persisted as the kiss lasted.

Ben's heart was torn between wanting to cling to this moment forever and knowing they had to let go. Hannah's touch electrified him, sending thrills down his spine. His fingers caressed her face, attempting to memorize every feature and curve. He wanted to remember this moment to be safe in his heart for the bleak days ahead.

"I will always cherish the love we shared, Ben," Hannah muttered. "You'll always be in my heart."

"And you'll always have a piece of my soul, my love," Ben almost choked.

Before letting go, Hannah said, "Promise me you'll take care of yourself?" she smiled, shaking. "Remember, you deserve happiness, too."

"I promise," he said, his voice hoarse. "I pray you find your joy."

Hannah smiled sadly and nodded. "I will," she murmured.

They parted. Their longing lasted.

A sense of finality enveloped the scene as he shut his car door. Tears streamed down Hannah's face as she smiled and waved him Goodbye.

Chapter 12

Truth Knocks

Ben stepped into his home, and the dimly lit living room suggested that chaos awaited. Fatigue couldn't prepare him for what the evening had yet to unveil.

As he entered the room, Sarah's gaze, once brimming with warmth and friendliness, now pierced him with raw abhorrence. She clutched a crumpled paper in her trembling hand, a shattering revelation set to destroy their world.

"What is this, Ben? Who is she? Did you write this for her?"

Ben's heart sank, and he tried to find the right words to explain.

"Sarah, I didn't mean for you to find that. I never wanted to hurt you."

Sarah trembled angrily, accusing Ben of betrayal.

He attempted to explain, but his voice faltered. Words could not calm Sarah's temper.

"Hurt me? Ha! Doing this behind my back?"

Ben's heart was muddled. Hannah was his true love, and he couldn't deny it. He tried to empathize with his wife, but it was in vain.

"I didn't plan for any of this to happen. It just ... happened. Love found me." Ben couldn't believe he said it.

"Love, my foot, Ben. I feel betrayed. How could you?" Sarah alternated between rage, hurt, and disappointment.

Ben's honesty shone through the argument. He loved Hannah but didn't want to upset Sarah.

"Do you love her?" Sarah asked in a firm voice.

Ben replied quietly, "Yes, I do … I love her, but that doesn't mean I don't care about our children.."

"You've made your choice, Ben, haven't you? You're leaving me for her."

Ben replied sadly, "I don't know what to say, Sarah. But I can't ignore my feelings. What do we have … huh? An empty, disrespectful, loveless life, bound by two other souls … how is this betrayal?"

Her voice trembled, and her eyes narrowed. "You seem to have no shame after cheating on me? After all we've been through together?"

Ben breathed deeply, searching for the proper words. "Sarah, I didn't mean to harm you. I've been feeling so lost lately; I met someone who ... understands me in a way I can't explain. Sometimes two good people are not so good together…"

Sarah's attitude changed from rage to astonishment. "Are you saying you're willing to throw it all away for a woman you barely know after everything we've built together?"

"Sarah, I don't know what to say. I haven't decided anything, but I know every life is precious, and we all deserve the chance to live. I've got mine, and I don't want to let it go. And I'm not saying I'm dumping my children or that I hate you … I … love her … I feel loved in her presence …"

Sarah's voice trembled with pain and anger. "Ben, you're selfish. You just think about yourself and what you desire. You're not considering our girls or our family."

Ben's eyes filled with tears as he attempted to explain. "I love our daughters, Sarah, but I can't deny how I feel. I can't pretend any more than I have that everything is okay between us when, clearly, it's not."

"How can you be so heartless?" Sarah's voice broke with emotion.

"Sarah, I don't think that it's me who is being selfish here."

Sarah's anger was amplified with truth thrown at her face, and she collapsed on the sofa, crying. "I thought we were happy. I thought we had something special."

"We did, but it didn't last; our partnership for a long time …. you know as much as I do that we drifted apart, and I've been lonely for years now," Ben said, attempting to comfort her.

Sarah brushed away her tears, her words laced with destitution. "You're pulling our family apart. You're breaking our hearts. How can you ever be happy?"

"I know, Sarah, and I'm so sorry," Ben whispered, with pain in his voice. "I care about my daughters and can't hurt them, but I deeply care about her, too."

Sarah needed someone to confide in and understand her stress. Thus, she contacted Ben's father to persuade him to change his ways.

Sarah invited Ben's father over. "I need to talk to you about something breaking me apart," she began.

Ben's father was attentive and worried. "Of course, Sarah. You can talk to me about anything. What's going on?"

Sarah chose to be honest after a bit of hesitation. "It's about Ben and this other woman he's involved with. I found a note, and when I confronted him, he admitted that he was in love with her."

Ben's father's expression tempered. "I felt Ben changing lately, and honestly, he seemed preoccupied & distracted, but he never opened up about it."

"I don't know what to do," Sarah murmured, tears welling up. "I can't stand the thought of him leaving me."

Ben's father softly replied, "I understand how difficult this must be for you, Sarah."

Sarah nodded, her emotions overtaking her. "It's hard to believe he could love someone else."

Ben's father suggested being honest and calm. "You need to talk and understand each other, Sarah. It's essential to know the difference. Love doesn't drift apart in the absence of pride."

Sarah swelled with anger. "So, you're implying that it's my pride that's hurt and not my love for him?!"

"You need to think with a calm head, is all I'm saying, and sort this out amicably. Sometimes, our happiness lies not in places we look."

Ben's father sat for a while and left without saying more.

***

"Sarah, I need to explain something to you," Ben said, taking a deep breath as they sat in their bedroom. The evening had yet to turn into night. "My emotions for Hannah are real, but I want you to know that it doesn't invalidate what we once had."

Sarah glanced at him angrily. "How long has it been … you having an affair with her?"

Ben concurred. "It began as a friendship and then developed into something more emotional. Despite my feelings for her, I care about our family."

Sarah stared down, pondering over his words. "Ben, I don't get it. What happened to us?"

"I am sorry. It's agonizing to go into details. I figured my part, Sarah; you'll have to figure yours," Ben murmured, touching and patting her hand.

***

A few weeks later, Sarah was diagnosed with breast cancer when she complained about a lump forming in her breasts. After checkups and tests, the news fell like a calamity upon Ben and their daughters. Sarah fought it with all her strength; her health had declined ever since the diagnosis, and she grew weak with time.

Ben, navigating a maze of intense emotions, remained steadfast in his devotion to look after his wife as she courageously fought her illness. This commitment, however, came with a heavy heart as he grappled with the reality of her illness and his love. Beside Sarah every day, Ben offered unwavering support, even as he wrestled with his own lonesomeness. The journey was a poignant reminder of the fragility of life and the strength that love and commitment hold, even amidst the deepest gloom.

The diagnosis had shaken him to the core, and he couldn't bear the thought of leaving her when she needed him the most.

However, his heart longed for Hannah, who had become his life's love in months.

***

He had not seen Hannah in five months, an insurmountable gap. The separation wore on him. His heart hurt every day.

Ben sat alone in the dimly lit bar at a corner table, sipping whisky. His shoulders fell, and his eyes empty. The deafening quiet in his head drowned out the laughing and talk around him.

A beautiful lady with a twinkle in her eye approached his table, her aroma filling the air as she murmured in his ear.

"Hey there, handsome. Mind if I join you?" she purred, pulling a chair.

Ben looked up, trying to muster a smile. "Sure, why not?" he replied, his voice lacking charm.

"I couldn't help but notice you sitting here all alone," she said, leaning closer. "You look like you could use some company."

He managed a half-hearted snicker. "You have no idea," he mumbled, sipping his drink.

She reached out and touched his arm gently. "Well, I'm here now. How about we have fun and forget our troubles for a while?"

Ben looked at her for a bit and accepted the offer. He needed the escape.

Ben's head was elsewhere as they danced to the music; he tried to bury himself in the moment, but his emotions were too sadistic.

The woman attempted to talk to him, feeling his distance. He responded vaguely to her questions about his life, hobbies, and passions. He would inadvertently compare every moment with this stranger to his time with the lady he loved.

As the night progressed, they sat snugly beside each other, her hand gently resting on his thigh, subtly drawing him nearer. Ben, however, guarded his heart, finding little solace in the embrace of the unfamiliar territory.

With a simulated smile, Ben excused himself to the restroom, a sanctuary to collect his scattered thoughts. In the solitude of the bathroom, he confronted his reflection in the mirror, a look of despair shadowing his features.

Upon returning to the table, a sense of guilt washed over him. He couldn't offer what she sought. Tenderly taking her hand apologetically, he said, "I'm sorry."

The lady nodded. "It's okay." Her gaze followed him till he left the bar with a combination of relief and remorse.

The transient diversions were too shallow to fill the vacuum inside him.

Strolling through the lonely streets in the chilly night air, he sought repair. Every moment, casting a shadow over his once lively spirit, he donned a mask of smiles, a feeble attempt to conceal the inner disarray slowly breaking him apart. A storm raged within him.

His daily routine loomed like an endless, monotonous battle. The zest for life that once defined him evaporated. His heart ached for Hannah. Yet, fate relentlessly erected barriers, feeding his soul with an all-consuming fear.

Ben's optimism faded as weeks turned into months. He wanted Hannah, but Sarah needed him.

He grieved alone, holding onto their memories.

After the longest five months, Ben's fingers shook as he began to write the message, his pulse hammering at each keystroke.

"Hello, Hannah, it's been a long time since we last talked; I wanted to check on you. I hope you're okay. I miss you ..."

The seconds seemed like hours as he anticipated her response.

Ben's pulse raced as Hannah's message finally popped up.

"Hello, Ben...I've missed you more than words can pronounce."

Ben read her measured words over and over again with tears in his eyes.

Ben: "I miss you so badly. These months have been torture without you. I think about you and us all the time."

Hannah: "Ben, not seeing or speaking to you has been difficult for me too."

The subsequent response stayed in Ben's head as he put the phone on his side and stared at the ceiling.

Chapter 13

A Glimmer

Hannah couldn't help but look for a way to distract herself. The dating app was a perfect idea. She spent her days scrolling through profiles. Adam caught her attention. They talked for a few days until he asked if they could meet in person, and Hannah in need for a change, agreed.

Adam asked about her interests, and she shared her passion for reading. But her eyes, usually radiant, held a touch of sadness as she spoke.

"So, Hannah, tell me about your interests. How do you spend your free time?"

"Well, I love to read," Hannah said quietly. "It lets me escape into other worlds and forget about my own."

"That's great!" Adam said. "What's the best book you've read that took you there?"

"Ha … um … I recently finished a beautiful novel about love and loss," Hannah said, trying to seem interested. "It's a bittersweet story that touched my heart."

"Sounds like an emotional read," Adam smiled. "I'm interested in hearing more."

As they continued talking, Hannah's mind wandered back to the last time she had shared deep conversations with Ben. She felt hollow, a hammer hitting her and somehow numbing her pain.

"Hannah, are you okay? You seem distant."

Hannah took a deep breath, "I'm sorry, Adam. I like your company, but I'm not sure I'm ready for this. My heart is still healing from a past love, and I don't want to lead you on."

"I understand," Adam said gently. "I appreciate your honesty. Healing takes time. I'm available if you want to speak or hang out as friends."

"Thanks, Adam," Hannah said as she picked up her jacket and bag to leave.

"Hey, let me walk you home…" It was more of a question. Hannah smiled and nodded. As the night drew to a close, Adam leaned in for a hug, and though his gesture was kind, all she could think about was the warmth and comfort of Ben's arms.

Hannah's hesitation embarrassed Adam, but he smiled and backed off gracefully.

"Sorry …"

"No, I'm sorry, Adam," Hannah said.

Adam gave a friendly hand gesture and turned to leave.

She felt terrible for not wholly embracing the possibilities of a new love.

Hannah's remaining walk home was a journey through a cascade of emotions, each step echoing with memories of Ben. As she moved through the city's glowing lights, they seemed to flicker with an eerie resemblance to the warmth she once found in Ben's presence. The stars above only intensified her longing.

In her efforts to grapple with an overwhelming hollowness, her heart battled between the urge to move on and the pain of missing her love. The adamant memories of Ben refused to fade into the backdrop of the city's night.

As the present became past, the hope stayed alive. Ben became like a lost jewel she still hoped to find.

She would mutter his name in the dark, thinking he might hear her. Every stride she made reminded her of her love that transcended time and place.

She courageously and vulnerably handled her recovery process, *or was she really recovering?*

She clutched onto her love like a guiding beacon in the dark until fate revealed a secret plan.

***

Hannah tapped her fingers anxiously at the quaint café.

"Hello, Hannah!"

Hannah almost jumped from her seat but pulled herself well, "Oh, hi, Alex."

"It's amazing to meet you in person finally. You're much more stunning than your photos."

Hannah flushed as a slight wave of nervousness came over her. "Thank you, Alex. I'll take that as a compliment, and it's nice to meet you, too."

Alex giggled as he sat back in his chair. "I was a little anxious about this date, honestly. You're easy to chat to, though."

His truthfulness made Hannah grin. "Thanks. I'm glad you feel that way."

"I guess I just have that effect on people," he replied jokingly, making Hannah laugh. "But really, I'm happy to be here with you."

They delved into a lighthearted banter, sharing stories about their favorite movies and most embarrassing moments. Alex seemed to know ways of bringing Hannah back from her lost love spams in the present moment.

He began to make her comfortable, and she opened up to him more than she anticipated.

"You know, I've been on a few dates from this app," Hannah revealed, "but I've never felt this comfortable with anyone before."

Alex's eyes softened with fondness. "Hannah, that's because you're awesome."

Hannah's heart leaped at his comment, and she momentarily forgot her misery. Alex made her feel special, something she had missed for a while.

They spoke about more serious things as the night wore on. Their bond grew stronger with time. Hannah was happy for Alex's diversion from her melancholy, laughing and smiling more than she had in a long time. They even discussed and debated the COVID-19 impact, the vaccination and life post pandemic.

***

Hannah couldn't think of dating other people. She could only think of Ben. After months, Alex finally succeeded in gaining her presence of mind.

She began to enjoy her hangouts with him but couldn't shake that feeling of emptiness yet. She yearned for the day when she would no longer miss Ben and would learn to live with the heartache.

She murmured to the cosmos, "I hope you're happy, Ben," thinking he might hear her. "I hope you've found peace and happiness."

Hannah sat there, sipping her coffee, lost in thoughts and recollections as the night grew darker. She understood mending would take time and that she had to be patient with herself. But until then, she would keep the memories of their love in her heart, cherishing the times they had spent and praying that someday, somehow, everything would fall into place. She silently hoped Ben can overcome the challenges of his situation and come back, ideally with his daughters' consensus.

She decided to write a text.

"Ben. How are you?"

She waited for his reaction for what seemed like an eternity. The suspense was intense, and her mind raced with possibilities of what he may say.

He responded.

"I've been okay. It's hard, but I'm taking care of my family and myself like any responsible man would."

His words sunk into Hannah's heart. She had learned about his wife's illness the last time they texted. It must have engulfed his life. She felt terrible for his burdening situation.

"I'm sorry for your hardship, Ben; I hope she's getting the best care, and you're taking care of yourself, too."

The conversation continued, and they exchanged updates on their lives. Hannah shared snippets of her work, friends, and attempts at moving on, minus Alex. Ben, in turn, spoke about the challenges he faced in his personal life and at work.

As they talked, Hannah couldn't help but feel a sense of comfort in their conversation. Even after all this time, there still was a connection beyond distance and time. It was bittersweet. On the one hand, she missed him so much, but on the other, she knew they couldn't be together.

"How have you been coping?" Ben asked, his words filled with concern.

Hannah paused before saying, *"It's been hard, Ben, if I'm honest. I miss you every day, but I'll be fine."*

"I miss you too, Hannah," Ben said. *"I think about us all the time."*

Hannah cried, reading his words. She wanted to say she loved him and wanted to be with him again, but she didn't. Their condition was tough to overlook.

"I wish things were different," she wrote. *"But we both made our choices and must live with the consequences."*

"I know," Ben said after a pause. *"I just want you to be happy, even if it means without me."*

His selflessness broke Hannah's heart. She wanted him to be selfish. Knowing he still loves her was comforting and painful at the same time. Nonetheless, it was like being free to choose another love. Could it be Alex?

"I want you to be happy, too, Ben," she said, with tears. *"I hope we both find the happiness we deserve."*

Their late-night talk included happy recollections and terrible truths. The second goodbye was hard, but not as hard as the first one, as they both knew better.

Overcome with emotion, Hannah placed her phone aside, tears, a testament to her heartache and a blissful outlet. In that moment of profound sorrow, she realized that her love for Ben, deep as it was, couldn't alter their fate.

This painful acceptance brought a bitter closure, etching a story of *love and loss* deep within her heart.

With a heavy pain in her chest, she whispered in the quietness of her room, "Goodbye, Ben."

Hannah tried to get on with her life. The agony of separation was a constant companion. Amid her work, hobbies, Alex, and friends, the ache in her heart never truly subsided. Ben's presence remained constant.

Chapter 14

Turning Hearts

The sun had begun to rise, casting a soft, warm glow across Ben's suburban home. The birds chirping outside seemed almost out of place in this quiet house filled with strain.

Ben moved about the kitchen with a practiced efficiency. Clad in his usual attire, a simple shirt and jeans that had seen better days, he expertly prepared breakfast, a routine he had come to better over the years. A tray was adorned with scrambled eggs, toast, and a small bowl of fruit salad. His daughters, Lily and Emma, were still upstairs in their rooms, likely lost in dreams of the day ahead, unaware of the story behind their father's barren heart.

As he moved about the kitchen, Ben couldn't help but steal glances at the bedroom door. Behind it lay his wife, Sarah, battling a disease that had cast a long shadow over their lives. The cancer had stolen her health and vitality, and COVID attacked her immune system exactly when she was most vulnerable, leaving her frail and in need of constant care.

Sickness had strangely altered Ben's relationship with Sarah. What was once a promising union eroded over the years, giving way to resentment and bitterness, was now a dignified patient and carer's bond. They stayed with each other for the sake of their daughters, but ailment merged them again.

An unspoken and ever-present truth lingered in the air. A truth that weighed heavily on Ben's shoulders and cast a shadow over his every action.

As he placed the finishing touches on the breakfast tray, he thought of Hannah and smiled. The woman who had captured his heart in a way he had never imagined possible and who he gave up on for his duty towards his daughters and his sense of guilt leaving them in pain to pursue his own happiness. She was the one who had shown him what it meant to be indeed alive, to have another chance in life, renewing his outlook to the future with a love so deep it shook him to his core.

But love, as he had understood, was a complex and often painful emotion. It could bind people together and tear them apart in the same breath.

Sighing, he picked up the tray and went to the garden. Lily, a bright-eyed thirteen-year-old with her mother's warm smile, sat by the water fountain. Her blue eyes lit up as she saw her father enter with the tray.

"Breakfast's here!" she exclaimed with a grin.

Ben ruffled her hair affectionately. "Yes, sweetie. Your sister will join us shortly."

Ben entered Emma's room. At ten, Emma was his Xerox image, with the same blue eyes and auburn hair.

He found her snuggling under the covers with her favorite stuffed bunny. Still half-asleep, her small frame barely visible beneath the colorful blanket.

Ben sat down beside her. "I prepared breakfast in the garden, sweety, just how you like it."

Emma's eyes brightened as she looked by the window of her room and saw the plate of pancakes topped with a generous dollop of whipped cream. It was her favorite, and Ben knew it well.

"Thanks, Daddy!" Emma exclaimed, jumping out of her bed running down the stairs to join her sister in the garden.

The two girls started eagerly digging into their breakfast. Ben watched them with a fond smile, savoring the precious moments with his daughters.

After breakfast, Ben helped Emma prepare for school, carefully braiding her hair and ensuring she had everything she needed for the day. Despite the challenges in his life, he remained a devoted and caring father to Lily and Emma, determined to provide them with as much love and support as humanly possible.

As he kissed Emma goodbye and watched her head off to school with her backpack bouncing, Ben couldn't help but feel joyful sadness.

***

Accompanied by her husband, Sarah went to the hospital for her routine checkup, the air tinged with nervousness and hope. *Hope is good; it keeps you going when you want to stop!* The waiting room, a familiar scene from countless visits, felt different this time. Ben felt it, too.

The receptionist greeted them pleasantly, and with a grateful smile, Sarah checked in for her appointment. In the examination room, she and Ben exchanged glances, a silent, somber understanding passing between them as they focused on the possibility of hopeful news.

The doctor entered with a warm smile and shared the news of Sarah's better recovery and the assurance that she would be out of danger soon. She had defeated COVID and almost Cancer. The C word haunted their lives for a time longer than anticipated. Relief washed over Sarah and Ben, and in that shared moment, Sarah's gaze at Ben expressed gratitude. Without Ben's care and sacrifice, the victory over adversity seemed far-fetched. Ben smiled at her quietly.

Leaving the hospital, Sarah and Ben walked side by side, the sunlight casting a glow on their shared journey. Sarah wanted to say goodbye to the wheelchair. The ride home became a space for reflection and gratefulness, which was enough for the moment.

It had been several weeks since Sarah discovered the seriousness of Ben's feelings for Hannah. They did not exchange any words on their ride home.

A few hours later, Ben found Sarah in the living room, sitting by the window, her gaze fixed on the world outside. He approached her cautiously.

"Ben," she began, her voice gentle, "Would you sit with me? I have important things to share with you."

He turned to look at her, his expression distant and apprehensive. "What's left to talk about, Sarah? I'm pleased you fought well and are again on the path to life."

Taking a deep breath, she mustered all her courage. "The pain we've caused each other is not unforgivable, Ben. But life has given me a second chance, and I want you to taste that, too. Please believe me, I've had time to reflect, and your feelings for Hannah no longer hurt me."

Ben looked at her like a child, surprised by their favorite gift. Sarah continued.

"Just bear with me and hear me out, please."

Ben nodded and sat beside her. After a brief calm, Sarah continued, "I chose you for love, Ben. Then, you gave me two beautiful flowers, and I know you love them even more than I can. Ben, Life is not short; we make it short with our egos …"

She paused to catch a breath. Ben offered water, but she gestured no.

"I never really knew when my love for you became an obsession. Everything life offered seemed to be my right. I felt accomplished, and that includes you, Ben. It was a mistake; I continued to enjoy that feeling of control until life came to teach me through Cancer and that too accompanied by COVID."

Ben patted her hand softly.

"If it weren't for you, I wouldn't be sitting here talking. You sacrificed your happiness to look after the mother of your children, who you didn't even love anymore …"

"Sarah ..."

"No, please let me finish, Ben. Whatever made me realize was successful and perhaps has left my body for now. I'm not saying I'll stop fighting it, but I'll be sharing a piece of your strength that you showed during all this time and will begin my life again in a different light. I am strong enough to set you *free* now for the love we once shared, but I will not be the other woman in your life. I won't resent it, but knowing you love another woman, I can't be with you. All I ask is a respectful friendship between us for the sake of our lovely daughters. Ben. I say this with an open heart; you're free to go."

"Sarah, I'm speechless. I don't know what to say except I feel very proud of you and respectfully grateful. But I'm not sure how Lily and Emma would feel about it."

"They are our daughters, Ben. I spoke with them two days before my appointment, and they cried until they got the point. They will always meet you with an open and respectful embrace."

"What? But they never showed a sign this morning!"

"They have their father's grace and their mother's strength, perhaps." Sarah smiled.

They shared a moment of light laughter after years.

Ben got up and hugged her gently, kissing her forehead.

"Sarah, you are a good woman, and I wish you a joy-filled life. I'll always be here when you need me, okay?"

"I know… now, go. We'll see you later."

Gesturing 'thank you' with a flying kiss, Ben rushed outside, feeling he was walking over the moon. The chains were broken, and the keys were handed to him with a smile. God loves love, doesn't he?

Sarah's health improved steadily in the following weeks, and she resumed her daily routines. But the emotional scars ran deep, and the trust that had once bound them together had been fractured. Only this time, she felt contended.

***

Hannah stood on the balcony of her cozy apartment, a cup of coffee in hand; she gazed out at the city below.

Over the past few months, Hannah had made a conscious effort to embrace life's simple pleasures. She had rekindled her love for photography, capturing the beauty of everyday moments through her camera lens. She had taken spontaneous road trips with her friends, exploring new places and creating lasting memories.

Today was another one of those days where she had planned a day trip with her closest friends, Cara, Amy, and Jake. They were heading to a picturesque countryside town renowned for its vibrant farmers' market and breathtaking hiking trails.

Hannah sipped her coffee, and she couldn't help but smile as she thought about the adventures that awaited her—moments like these allowed her to forget the ache in her heart.

"Ready to roll?" Amy's cheerful voice interrupted Hannah's thoughts as she entered the balcony, already dressed in comfortable hiking attire.

Hannah turned to her friend and nodded, setting her coffee cup aside. "Absolutely!"

With that, the three friends embarked on their day trip, leaving behind the worries and heartaches of the past. They laughed, shared stories, and immersed themselves in the simple joys of the present.

Although Hannah was trying to move forward, she couldn't help but carry a piece of Ben wherever she went. She often glanced at her phone, hoping for a message that never came.

But for now, she focused on her friends' company, relishing the sun's warmth on her skin and the beauty of the world around her. Each moment was a step towards healing, a reminder that life was still worth living, even without the one person who had held her heart.

Jake, Cara, and Amy were a blessing in Hannah's life. She couldn't have asked for better friends, always there whenever she felt low. A little trip at this time of her life was nothing short of a gift. Their day in the countryside was magical. They wandered through the bustling farmers' market, sampling fresh produce, artisanal cheeses, and delectable pastries. Hannah's camera was always ready, capturing the vibrant colors and smiling faces surrounding her.

After indulging in a hearty picnic under the shade of a sprawling oak tree, Hannah with her friends set off on a hike along a scenic trail that led to a hidden waterfall. The rushing water and the cool mist on their faces filled them with wonder and contentment.

As they sat by the waterfall, sharing stories and laughter, Hannah couldn't help but feel grateful for her friends, offering comfort and understanding without judgment.

Yet, beneath the laughter and camaraderie, there lingered an unspoken truth.

The rushing water created a soothing backdrop as they sat by the waterfall, and their conversation turned reflective.

Jake's gaze fixed on the cascading water broke the silence first. "Hannah, you've been through so much and handled it with such grace. Not everyone can do that."

With a wistful smile, Hannah traced her fingers through the cool mist rising from the falls. "Thank you, Jake. I couldn't have done it without friends like you and Cara."

"Hello!" Amy frowned as they all laughed.

Cara, sitting closer to Hannah, reached out and squeezed her hand. "We're here for you, you know that, right?"

Hannah nodded, her voice soft, "I do. And I appreciate it more than I can say."

The conversation tapered into a comfortable silence as they took in the moment's serenity.

Hannah finally said, "You know, guys, sometimes I wonder if I'll ever be able to move on completely."

"Hannah, it's okay to take your time. Healing isn't linear," said Amy gently.

Jake added, "And you don't have to rush into anything. When the right person comes along, you'll know."

Hannah sighed, "I hope so. But right now, I'm just trying to enjoy moments with you guys. You mean the world to me."

They shared a knowing look, the unspoken truth hanging in the air.

The four friends returned to the city as the sun descended in the sky. The day had been a welcome respite from the bustle in Hannah's heart, although only a reprieve.

Chapter 15

Will You?

In the quiet moments before sleep claimed her nights, Hannah often thought about Ben, wondering if he ever felt the same longing and emptiness as she did. She couldn't know for sure, but she clung to the hope.

In the weeks that followed their countryside excursion, Alex continued to be a persistent presence in Hannah's life. His genuine and patient approach to pursuing her was a source of comfort amid her emotional chaos.

One sunny afternoon, as they sat in Hannah's favorite café, 'The Cozy Cafe,' sipping on cappuccinos and sharing stories, Alex couldn't help but notice the thoughtful expression on Hannah's face. He knew that her heart still bore the scars of a past love, and he had no intention of pushing her to move faster than she was ready.

"Hannah," he began, his tone gentle, "I want you to know I'm here for you. I enjoy spending time with you, and I care about you deeply. But I also understand that healing takes time, and that's perfectly okay."

Hannah looked at him, her eyes filled with gratitude. "Alex, you have no idea how much your friendship means to me. You've been patient and understanding, and I can't thank you enough."

He smiled, his warm brown eyes meeting hers. "It's the least I can do, Hannah. You're an incredible person, and you deserve nothing but the best. I'll be here whenever you're ready to take the next step."

Alex noticed a hint of sadness in Hannah's eyes. He decided to change the mood.

"Hey, you know what?" he said with a mischievous grin. "I've got a surprise for you."

Hannah raised an eyebrow, her curiosity piqued. "A surprise? What is it?"

Alex leaned in closer, his voice filled with excitement. "Well, I know you love art, and this incredible art exhibit is happening downtown. It's supposed to be mind-blowing. What do you say we check it out?"

Hannah's eyes lit up with surprise and delight. "An art exhibit? I'd love to, Alex!"

They quickly finished their cappuccinos and made their way to the art exhibit. As they strolled through the gallery, Hannah's spirits began to lift. The vibrant colors, intricate details, and thought-provoking art pieces were a welcome distraction from the world's complexities.

Alex was right by her side, offering insights, sharing stories, and making her laugh with his witty remarks. He had a way of turning even the most somber moments into ones filled with joy.

As they reached a particularly striking painting, Alex turned to Hannah with a playful twinkle in his eye. "You see this one? It's like the artist painted the colors of happiness itself."

Hannah couldn't help but smile. "You have a way of making everything look brighter, Alex."

He grinned, his eyes locked on hers. "Well, that's my life's secret mission: to bring a little more light into the world."

At that moment, as they stood amid art and laughter, Hannah felt a deep gratitude for having someone like Alex in her life. While her heart still carried the weight of her past love, she was learning that healing could come in unexpected ways through the kindness and companionship of a true friend.

As days turned into weeks, Hannah's internal conflict continued to wage war on her. She had tried to move forward, to give herself a chance at happiness with someone new, but her heart remained tethered to Ben.

One sunny afternoon, as Hannah sat with Alex in a charming cafe, she couldn't help but admire his genuine kindness. He was always there for her, offering comfort and a listening ear whenever needed. His unwavering care had become a beacon of light in her life.

As they chatted about their plans for the weekend, Alex reached across the table and took Hannah's hand in his. She looked at him with a warm smile.

"Hannah," he began, his voice steady but filled with emotion, "there's something I've meant to say."

Hannah looked at him in the eyes, waiting for him to continue.

Alex's gaze was unwavering, his eyes locked onto hers. "Hannah, I can't help but feel that I've known you forever, even though it's only been a short time. You've brought so much light into my life."

He continued with a deep breath; his words carried the weight of his emotions. "I love you, Hannah. I've loved you since we met, and every moment I've spent with you has deepened that love."

Hannah's heart fluttered at his confession. She sensed his affection for her, but hearing *I love you* spoken aloud was shocking.

"Alex, I..." she started, her voice trembling, torn between her lingering feelings for Ben and the kind, caring man before her.

He continued, his words filled with sincerity, "I know you've been through a lot, and your heart carries the weight of the past. But I want to be there for you, Hannah. I want to make you happy and cherish every moment together."

And then, in a moment that caught her by surprise, Alex reached into his pocket and pulled out a small velvet box. He opened it to reveal a beautiful, sparkling ring.

"Hannah," he said, his voice filled with hope, "Will you marry me?"

Hannah's eyes filled with tears as she looked at the ring and then back at Alex. Though entangled in a web of emotions and conflicted desires, her heart was soaring.

In that intimate café corner, surrounded by the gentle melody of the breeze and the fabulous glow of sunlight, Hannah saw the possibility of a new chapter in her life. Her heart, once burdened by the past, was beginning to open up to the warmth of love once more.

"Will you?"

Their emotional gazes met and spoke volumes. However, Hannah just said one word, "Yes!"

Chapter 16

Bittersweet

New York seemed even brighter today. Ben drove at a speed he'd never driven before. He wanted to accelerate the time and hug Hannah so tight, revealing the best news of their life: *they were going to be together!*

Although he couldn't wait to reach her, he stopped for her favorite yellow tulips and coffee from her favorite café. Ben didn't even realize the smile never left his face since he embarked in his long but so exciting drive to New York. He parked and rushed to the counter of 'The Cozy Café' to take two Caramel Frappuccinos for the go. He smiled and gave a hefty tip to the sweet counter staff and responded as he turned quickly, "You too, buddy, have a great, lovely day."

The world seemed so beautiful suddenly … almost perfect.

As he stepped out of the café, his eyes turned to the right, and his perfect world came crumbling down just like the two Caramel Frappuccinos from his hands. Hannah and Alex turned to look at the noise, and Hannah froze in her place.

"Hannah, Hannah!"

"Huh."

She woke up from a nightmare as Alex's fingers before her face tried bringing her to come out of the trance.

"Are you okay, Hannah?"

"I … umm … yeah, yes, I'm good. Let's go …"

She grabbed her bag and walked without looking back. Alex caught up.

***

Ben didn't know how long he sat in the car before driving back home. The world that was glowing all the way seemed so deserted now. Hannah had found her joy, and he was late. A part of him felt happy for her, and the other part was shattered in pieces. But this was fate's script, and he had no choice but to accept it. At least he could get there; the chains were broken, but he'd lost the battle with time.

Days passed by, and the thought of Hannah with another man and the realization that he needed to confront his feelings had kept him loaded. Ben was spending his nights in agony, recalling every detail, and with it every painful emotion, of the terrible moment of truth in the café. The nights grew even darker and heavier, till he decided he couldn't wait any longer.

Ben quietly slipped out of bed with a heavy heart, careful not to wake his daughters, and padded down the hallway to Sarah's room. Moonlight filtered through the curtains, casting a faint glow in the dimly lit room. Sarah was asleep, her breathing steady and deep. Ben stood there for a moment, watching her peaceful form. He couldn't help but feel a pang of guilt for what he was about to do. But he knew it was necessary.

Ben's nightly ritual of checking Hannah's social media accounts had become a joy for him. Though Hannah rarely shared her private life on these platforms, one momentous evening, as he continued his search, he stumbled upon a picture from Cara, her close friend. Cara had tagged Hannah in a photo that threatened to steal his breath. Hannah stood radiant and joyous in that photograph, her hand adorned with a glistening ring, standing by the handsome man he saw in the cafe.

Ben's heart felt like it had been plunged into icy water. He desperately wanted to believe it was a bad dream; Hannah was building a future with someone else. His emotions were a turbulent storm of happiness for her and an overwhelming sense of loss for himself.

Ben's heart sank as he stared at the image, a stark reminder that the woman he had loved, the woman he still loved, was moving forward with her life with another man.

At that moment, something inside him snapped.

As Ben gazed at her photo, he knew he had to tell her. With a deep breath, he held his phone …

Ben: *Dear Lady Hannah, it's been a while. I saw you're doing well. I'm happy for you. Sarah is now well, and Emma and Lily understand the matters of my heart. My heartfelt wishes are always with you. I'm forever grateful for us. Thank you …"*

He pressed send, and as he waited, he wondered if his message would finally bring clarity to the tangled web of emotions that had trapped them for so long.

He had reached out to Hannah, a step he had never imagined taking until he saw that picture of her radiant and happy self with her new found love. He couldn't deny it any longer; his feelings for Hannah were as strong as ever, and her impending marriage had ignited a firestorm of doubts and regrets.

Was it fair on his part to contact her now and disrupt her happiness? What if she was doing just fine without him?

Ben knew that the right thing to do, now, the honorable thing, was to let Hannah go with what she had chosen after all.

***

Hannah looked radiant in her engagement dress, and Alex was a brilliant dancer. The floor was theirs after the beautiful intimate engagement ceremony that their friends organized for them. Amy, Jake, and Cara were by Hannah's side. Alex had his share of friends, too.

The music, dance, food, and the joy of laughter. Hannah was finally happy. As Alex had a moment with his friends, Hannah looked for her clutch to check her phone, which worried her and made her doubt her feelings. Hannah's heart raced as she saw Ben's message. It was as if a floodgate of emotions had burst open, and she struggled to navigate the turbulent waters of her feelings. She closed the clutch and turned back but couldn't stop opening it again. Every word was a strike straight into her heart. Especially, *'Emma and Lily understand the matters of my heart!'*

His words echoed in her mind. She couldn't deny that a part of her waited for an eternity to hear something like this, and it came on her very engagement day! *Wow, Ben, Bravo!*

126

But now that he shared the news with her, it was as if he had unleashed Pandora's box of emotions.

Anger welled up inside her. She didn't blame Ben for their separation, but for not fighting harder and earlier to be with her. Which had broken her heart. She wanted to lash out, to tell him that it was too late, that he had missed his chance.

But beneath the anger was a deep yearning. Hannah had tried to move on and give her heart to Alex, the kind and patient man. But did she? She had given him her time, smiles, and agreement, but her heart had been long taken. Was it fair to Alex? A tornado within her escalated.

She wrote back.

Hannah: *Hi Ben, thank you for reaching out. I appreciate your kind words. I wanted to talk to you about something as well. I've met someone, and we've become close. We're engaged now. I hope you can understand that I've chosen to move forward with my life. I wish you the best, too.*

Chapter 17

It's Not The Mind

Ben couldn't sleep that night, and neither could Hannah.

The doorbell was the last thing she wanted to hear, but she knew it was Alex and had to answer.

"Hannah, are you okay?"

"I'm fine, Alex; why?"

You went quiet after the dance and didn't join us for the celebratory dinner. All the friends missed you."

"I'm sorry, Alex, I had this great nausea, something I ate…"

Alex hugged her and took her by surprise.

"Hannah, you are a treasured one, and as much as I've known you in the last few months, you will break your own heart but not anyone else's. But remember, we were friends before we decided to marry. If something disrupts your mind, you can tell me without inhibitions, okay?"

"Alex, why are you always so sweet to me?"

"Because your vibe is such, one can only be sweet to you, my lady." Hannah couldn't help but smile at his acting gesture.

After a brief silence, Hannah spoke in a serious tone, "Alex, I can't keep you in the dark … It's not my mind … it's my heart!"

Alex straightened up and looked into her eyes. He spoke in a measured tone, "So, it's Ben, right?"

Hannah looked down and nodded.

"He wants to be back in your life?"

"He never left, Alex. He just broke the chains too late."

"Hannah…. What matters is what your heart wants, and before you answer, know that I'm with whatever you decide."

Hannah stared crying like a baby as Alex held her. Moments passed, and he continued caressing her back, hiding his disappointment and hurt. All he knew was she deserved the joy of her heart. She should *never* have to suffer.

"I'm so sorry, Alex … I …"

"Shhh … it's okay. I know that you and Ben go deeper than our bond. But as friends, don't you dare rank him up, ever, right?"

Hannah finally laughed and hugged him tight.

'Thank you.' She lip-synced, and he reciprocated with a flying kiss …

"What about our families and friends, Alex?" the innocent concern on her face made him smile.

"Leave it to me; it's been a while since I had a serious job," he winked as he turned to leave.

***

Ben slowly slipped out of bed with a heavy heart, thinking of his daughters. He padded down the hallway of his hotel, where he decided to stay for a while after he announced the separation to his daughters and agreed to spend as much time with them as possible during week-ends and after school on week days. He already initiated the process of joint custody and was progressing with the divorce papers.

He knew Sarah would be asleep at this hour, and he wondered how his life would be after he traveled back the next day, knowing his divorce would be final soon, but he was now at peace that it would be amicable. Sarah and Ben would always be friends and co-parents of their daughters. Only he would never be able to fill Hannah's void.

He looked at the clock. It was 9:30 PM. The Cozy Café wouldn't close till 11:30 PM. He needed some fresh air; he decided to drive all the way, just to feel close and sit at the same table Hannah used to choose and have her favorite coffee.

****

Disenchantment with an unshakeable sense of failure dominated his thoughts and feelings and streamed down his face as he sipped his coffee. It smelled of his Hannah.

He didn't know how long had passed since he sat with his head down, his coffee now cold.

"More coffee, sir?"

Ben jumped at the sound. He looked up and couldn't believe his eyes. With her sparkling eyes and out-of-the-world smile, Hannah stood with her hands folded.

"Good God, please, no more trials. Is it you, Hannah?"

"No, it's my ghost craving for my favorite coffee, which is now taken, I see."

Ben reached out and gently held her hand with a serious yet priceless expression, with thousands of silent questions reflecting in his eyes. She hugged him gently and patted his back. She then touched his lips and spoke in the softest whisper ever, "Ben, now is finally the time to smile, my love."

"But ..."

She cut him off with her finger on his lips. "But Alex, too, understands the matters of *my* heart," she smiled.

"Oh, Hannah, I can't believe I could be so lucky!"

"It's fate, Ben. And Fate is the best script writer."

"You want to walk under the bright sky and thank fate?" Ben finally smiled, a smile he'd long forgotten.

"Yes, Ben, I want to feel that tonight will never end with the two of us reunited again by fate". "But I have a wish" she said, I wish to see Sarah with yellow tulips and embrace Emma and Lily… can I?" Of course Hannah, I'm so happy you want to see them" said Ben with a relieving joy as they walked under the bright sky that looked repainted for them in this magical night, long dreamed of but doubtfully expected to happen.

The precipice of choices, patience, love, and sacrifice finally redefined their destinies. As Covid suggested, 'distances broke distances!'

The Beginning

www.ingramcontent.com/pod-product-compliance
Lightning Source LLC
Chambersburg PA
CBHW040830010826
48978CB00012BB/692